Copyright © 2020 by Matilda Martel

All rights reserved. No part of this book may be reproduced or transmitted in any form, including electronic or mechanical, without written permission from the publisher, except in the case of brief quotations embodied in critical articles or reviews.

This is a work of fiction. Names, characters, businesses, places, events, and incidents are either the products of the author's imagination or used in a fictitious manner. Any resemblance to actual persons, living or dead, or actual events is purely coincidental.

This book is licensed for your personal enjoyment only.

Cover by Avdal Designs

Want a free Ebook? Join my mailing list to get my monthly newsletter!

Love redeems us all

LUCIFER

FALLEN ANGELS, BOOK ONE

MATILDA MARTEL

1
LUCIFER

"You've been a bad boy, Arthur."

The sniveling piece of filth who summoned my presence with his murderous misdeeds, stares slack-jawed at the dark wings unfurling through the seams of my overpriced suit. The look of terror on his previously smug face delights me.

"Who..." He swallows hard and urinates in his tight-fitting sweatpants. "Are you?"

I raise an eyebrow and stare in disgust at the yellow puddle pooling at his feet. "Don't insult me. You know exactly who I am."

"Sa... Sa...Sa... tan?" He stammers and sprays the air with his saliva.

I reach into my breast pocket and retrieve a silk handkerchief. With a wave of my hand, I send this poor excuse for human excrement flying into the concrete wall on the other side of the room. As I pat my forehead, removing evidence of his rancid spittle, I watch him scramble to his feet and sprint towards the only exit.

He pulls the handles, swings the doors wide and runs straight into my chest. His high-pitched scream is almost as loud as the primal cries of mercy that fueled his twisted bloodlust thirty minutes ago. *Almost.*

"I prefer Lucifer. Satan is simply what I do. I am your adversary. And let me be clear. I am your enemy." I push his foul, sweaty body away and he falls to the floor.

His pale face contorts as he gasps for air. Sliding backwards on his ass, he stammers as he cries. "Why are you here?"

I take a deep breath, bring my finger to my lips and pretend to think. "Did you know the woman you just killed taught preschool?"

His eyes widen. "No. I didn't." He sobs and clasps his hands to plead for his life.

I wave a dismissive hand. "Stop that. You don't expect me to be more merciful than you. Do you? Make no mistake, Arthur. You are moments away from a painfully gruesome death that I will thoroughly enjoy."

He shrieks and tries to crawl away. Chuckling to myself, I jump on the back of his calves and hear the familiar snap of breaking bones. When he wails louder, I clamp his mouth shut.

I swear, I can't hear myself think.

"She was twenty-five years old and fresh out of school. She'd wanted to be a teacher all her life, Arthur. Would you care to know why she was out tonight? I think I'll tell you. She went out to buy a sketchbook for a little boy who's been so traumatized by his abusive father, he refuses to speak. Sounds like a nice girl, doesn't it? I thought you'd think so." I step onto his hand, twist my foot and shatter it. Thankfully, the steel patch glued to his face muffles his cries.

I continue. "She had parents who loved her. She had students who relied on her. Helen Butler was a decent person who tried to make this detestable world a better place. She didn't deserve to be violated. She didn't deserve eight stab wounds. But you know who does?"

I pull a machete out of thin air and bend to take his face in my hands. "Don't answer that. It doesn't matter anymore. Your life is over, Arthur." I gently slap his tear-stained face.

Sliding my hand into his hair, I grip his greasy locks and pull. "This is your third kill in two months. Time's up." I take my time. No quick deaths for men like him. With a slow, messy slice, I separate his sinful head from his broken body.

Stifling a smile, I watch his shell-shocked soul retreat into Purgatory. There, he'll wait to be reborn. Another chance to prove his worthiness to God.

Good riddance.

I know what you're thinking. What took me so long? Why didn't I save Helen Butler?

That's not my job. I have no skin in your game. Like all angels, I do what I'm told and play my part. There can be no interference in the fate of the righteous.

But once you sin, your ass is mine.

Believe me, Helen's in a much better place. Unlike Arthur, who will continue to relive one horrible life after the next, Helen has reached the upper echelons of heaven where she'll remain for eternity.

Few are so lucky. *I certainly wasn't.*

I was once the Archangel of Light. God's perfect creation. Most beautiful and beloved above all others. My sin was pride. I never lusted for human women. I never taught sorcery or war. Yet, unlike you, the wages of my sin are everlasting.

No forgiveness.

No second chance.

I've spent thousands of years perched on my earthly throne, watching you live debauched, unsavory lives with no regard for the consequences.

Your weaknesses disgust me. Your flaws infuriate me. You sin, you repent, and our heavenly father welcomes you back with open arms.

MATILDA MARTEL

I will never understand what he sees in you.

2
LUCIFER

IT IS BETTER TO REIGN IN HELL THAN SERVE IN HEAVEN.

I didn't say that. Those are Milton's words. I lead this lost paradise because I was the first to fall. I never led an army of heavenly rebellion, and I never visited the Garden of Eden. I'm just a cautionary tale that failed to dissuade others from following in my path.

Despite what you've heard, I don't desire your praise or adoration. Your scattered worship amuses me. Your contempt bores me and your scorn is inconsequential. In the beginning, the power and illusion of control soothed my wounded pride. But that faded quickly.

There is no comparison to living in the light.

I want to be free. I want to go home. I've requested an audience with Father for ages, but he won't speak to me. Any possible redemption hinges on the only creature I dislike more than humans. My brother, Michael. Only he can deliver my pleas.

I know my betrayal wounded him. But he must have known my fate from the moment he created me. Why was I chosen for this?

Before I was shunned from the light, my love was true. My worship unrivaled.

I don't understand why he won't forgive me.

"You requested my presence, little brother?" As I watch over a sinful pastor on the verge of committing grand larceny, Michael appears beside me. His pristine robes match the pompous air that floats around him.

"Cut that out. We're the same age. When did the old man let you start reading my mind?" I look down my nose at his smug face and try to calm the beat of my racing heart. I'm not capable of feeling physical injury or illness, and yet the sight of him makes me sick.

"I have my ways. A little bird tells me you still seek redemption. What makes you think Father will change his mind after all this time?"

I release an audible groan. There's no excuse for my sin. I admit I was foolish to crave adulation. But why the hell does his arrogance remain unchecked?

He stares into a window across the street and eyes the sweaty man of God sitting hunched over his laptop. "Do you really think he'll go through with it?"

I nod. "Yes. He needs to pay off his mistress before she blabs to his entire congregation that her son is his. Coming clean would cost him his position and marriage. He's decided this is the lesser offense."

He frowns. "That makes no sense."

I shrug and squat to get a closer look. "They make little sense. They only think in terms of now. Not tomorrow. Not eternity."

"Why do you hate them so much? It's not good for you. Father loves them. We should too." He sits next to me and hangs his legs over the ledge.

"That's *his* story. Their lives are constant torment and their devotion brings them no relief. The more rotten they are, the more blissful their lives become. He could and should reward them accordingly." I immediately regret my words. If I say too much, I'll lose my chance.

He sighs and to my surprise, nods. "He works in mysterious ways. He loved you once. He must still have a place for you in his heart. But what makes you believe you're worthy of forgiveness?"

"Worthy? I've done what was asked. I wallow with the dregs of society. If I've been tainted by their wickedness, it's his fault." I growl and imagine closing my hands around his self-righteous neck.

"Everything you do, you do for you. You don't seek heavenly justice. Your vengeance satisfies your rage. In seven thousands years, you have yet to perform one selfless act." He stands and shakes off his wings, creating a small cloud of feathers and dust.

"That's not true…" I anger at the implication but I can't counter him with evidence to the contrary.

"But I know you've been treated unfairly. I will intercede on your behalf. Perhaps there is a task you can perform." He smirks with condescension.

My ears perk. "A task? What sort of task?" I hide my enthusiasm for fear this is another prank at my expense.

"I'll find you when I know more. Take care, brother."

3
LIVIA

IF YOU COULD SEE WHAT I SEE, YOU WOULD KNOW YOU'RE never alone.

From an early age, I knew I wasn't normal. Normal people don't see what I see. They don't know what I know. I accept it. Normal will never know my address. With no other option, I embrace this strange existence as my only reality.

My grandmother always said we De Lucio's come from the light. Descended from angels who coupled with human women, we carry light within us that lets us see what others cannot.

A gift from our ancestors.

My father didn't agree. It was his curse. For years he fought it. Psychiatrists. Therapists. Mental health facilities. Meditation retreats in the Blue Ridge Mountains. By the time he was thirty, he was certain he'd lost his mind. For his own safety, doctors kept him so medicated, he spent all day every day numb to the world. And yet, the voices and visions never went away.

Desperate, he turned to booze and drugs. Anything to quiet the noise. If that ever helped, his reprieve from insanity was brief. Days after his thirty-third birthday, he drowned out the noise for good.

You can't see or hear anything locked in a carbon steel casket six feet underground.

I don't know if it's a gift or a curse, I just know I've always had it. My father hoped my mother's blood would dilute his own, but before I could utter a word, he knew he'd failed.

Angels hovered near my crib when I was months old. They watched me take my first steps. Throughout my childhood, they guided me with words and ethereal light that pointed me in the right direction. But ever-present, was the promise that darkness would eventually drag me into the abyss. I feel it hovering over me like a fate I can't escape.

Whatever it is. Whatever it becomes. I won't end like my father. I won't let this beat me.

"Are you meeting a boyfriend in Rome?" The slick man seated next to me does his best impression of an Italian gigolo. His oily dishwater blond hair and weak chin compliment his smudged dark-framed glasses. They're not real. He's using fashion lenses to disguise his features and make himself seem approachable. But a sinister aura surrounds him.

I ignore his comment and curl my body towards the window. While he pretends to read a travel magazine, his mind churns with thoughts of Rome, skimpy lingerie and the collection of knives he's brought in his checked luggage. I'm not sure if he's ever killed before, but he has clear aspirations of starting with me.

"Is your boyfriend Italian?" His odd accent catches me by surprise. I furrow my brow and stare bewildered into the seat in front of me. He's not Italian. He's an American imitating an Italian accent and moments from telling me he'd be happy to show me around Rome.

"No, I'm traveling for work. Thank you." I lift my book to cover my face and pray he drops it.

"No one works all day. Allow Gianni to show you his city.

You'll love evenings in Roma." He smiles and leans into my seat, stunning me further. His creep factor is through the roof and his accent is truly offensive. Some of my closest friends were born in Italy and none have ever referred to themselves in the third person.

"I work for the Holy See. The Pope's schedule never stops. This isn't my first trip to Rome." I scribble a few notes and ignore him calling me a *bitch* under his breath.

Faint laughter floats from behind our seats, drifting in the air like voices carried through the breeze. The distinctive timbre of an otherworldly voice is striking. In my peripheral, I spot a dark angel and guardian quietly arguing the man's merits as a flight attendant passes through them with the final beverage cart.

I flinch at the sight. Guardians are always present, but the fallen rarely make such bold appearances. He looks like the rest. But unlike his guardian friend, his wings are gray and his light is dimmed by a murky veil of pain.

The creep's guardian struggles to name his qualities. He sounds defeated and his light wavers as he tries to convince the man beside me not to take this wicked path. The demon doesn't do much to swing him in the opposite direction. He's here to bear witness to a scene. We're in the midst of this man's fall from grace, and I've been selected to play an active role.

I don't think so, gentleman. This won't be my fate. They don't know I can hear them. They can't fathom that someone like me still exists.

When the man's thoughts slip further into darkness, I grow tired of their uselessness. If my own guardian can't intervene, I'll do it myself. Scouting the area, I slam the button overhead. The flight attendant ignores the bell, so I hit it again. A handsome man in the front row has her undivided attention. She's too busy lining up a possible sugar daddy to concern herself with the frantic girl in 3C.

Frightened that the man sitting next to me is a serial killer in the making, I silently scream her name in my mind. The laughter behind me ceases. Two rows ahead, the attendant jolts her head up and finally catches my stern gaze.

"Signorina De Lucio, do you require another beverage?" She takes my empty glass and waits for my response.

"What gate are we landing in? I need to notify the Gendarmes when we land. They'll be waiting for me."

The creep stiffens. His features contort as his brain deciphers this new information. If the mention of military police doesn't set him straight, nothing will.

"And I'd love some seltzer and lime. *Grazie mille.*" I answer with a chirp. Predators feed on fear and I don't want this psychopath to grow bold. With a nod and a smile, the attendant rushes away to complete my request.

"I apologize for bothering you." He mumbles and takes a sip of whiskey. While his mind returns to calm things that do not include slicing my throat and throwing my limp body in the Tiber, his sudden remorse catches both angels off guard.

The pair argues. The guardian rejoices at Lionel's, *not Gianni's*, decision to walk away. But the demon is unconvinced.

"He didn't have a change of heart. He walked away out of fear and self-preservation. Someone like him will change his mind before the end of the day. At best, this is a draw." The angel with dark wings shakes his head and bats Lionel's hair. His hand goes through his skull like a gust of wind, startling my gaze towards him. Our eyes meet briefly before I turn away. It's too late, his awareness is instant.

He knows I see him. With his eyes glued to me, he nudges the guardian and points. "She saw me. That girl knows we're here."

"Don't be ridiculous. Try showing grace in defeat." It's hard to ignore their chatter, but I duck my head back into my book and manage. This isn't the first time an angel suspects my sight. It's clear humans aren't meant to see them in their natural state. And yet, I do.

Arguing like school children, they push each other down the short aisle, shaking off feathers that no one else can see. Just before they head out into the sky through the plane's aluminum body, the demon cranes his head in my direction and winks.

What have I done?

4

LUCIFER

As the sun peeks over the horizon, I step onto the terrace to survey the city below. There's beauty in darkness. The night sky hides the flaws and imperfections that daylight reveals. On the 125th floor, everyone's faceless and flawless. There is no crime. No noise or pain. No glaring sins to judge. Soon the sun will destroy the façade and bring the ugliness to light.

"Have you heard?" Stomping boots break my reverie. Gray feathers dance across my line of sight and almost land in my snifter of brandy.

It's Azazel, forth in the line of seniority after Samael, Asmodeus, and, of course, me. He's great at keeping the others in line, but he's the biggest busybody I've ever met.

"Samael's in love?" I take a sip and wait. That question hardly deserves an answer. The possibilities are endless.

"No, that's old news." He shakes his head simultaneously fluttering his wings, then steps closer.

"Malphas is being mean to you?" I take another stab.

"Let me finish my damn sentence. I promise you'll want to

know more." He wipes his sweaty brow and leans into the stone ledge.

"Continue." I rest an elbow on the ledge and gesture for him to speak.

"Amon swears he met a woman who sees." He folds his massive arms on his chest, satisfied that he's given me enough information.

My eyes narrow with annoyance. "And? Sees what? You never shut up and now you decide to be cryptic?"

"Sees us! What do you think she sees? Santa Claus? She sees us. She can see into our world." He scratches his beard and sighs. "She saw Amon. He doesn't have the power to reveal himself in his natural form. And yet she saw him. How?"

I stare, speechless, genuinely unsure of how to respond. That doesn't seem possible. Unless we allow it, only angels can see angels. "How does he know? Did she speak to him?"

"No. They made eye contact." He explains.

"I'm not sure I trust Amon. You're talking about a human with true sight. Why haven't we heard about her? Someone with those gifts would have caught our radar by now." I tilt my head and wait for him to defend his lackey.

"Normally, I wouldn't either." He surprises me. "But he swears she looked him right in the eye. He said he felt her in his mind. In this case, I believe him."

"In his mind? Does she read thoughts?" My curiosity piques. Can she read ours?

"They didn't chat. He just said he felt her in his mind. He's watching her and waiting for you in Rome." He points to the east as if we can see Italy from my terrace.

"Waiting for me? Surely, someone else can verify. I'm surprised someone upstairs hasn't caught wind and plotted her premature death." I button my jacket and check my watch. "What time is it in Rome?"

He shrugs. "Early afternoon. Just add six hours to your watch."

He's one of my oldest friends, so I occasionally indulge his sarcasm. Perhaps I've been too lenient.

"This better not be a waste of time." My voice grates with irritation as I jump on the ledge and draw a fiery door. As much as I'd like to spread my wings, I'm not flying to Europe.

Amon better be right.

If he wants to keep his head, he better be right.

5
LIVIA

"Livia, how was your flight?" Cardinal Ciro Lunetta greets me with outstretched hands and offers me a seat in his cluttered office. While I set my bags in a clean corner, I glance back and forth between two chairs piled with books, unsure which one he means.

"Almost uneventful. I witnessed a temptation for the first time in years. When we're done, I'd like to speak to the Inspector General about a pressing concern. A man seated next to me on the flight has murderous intentions for his stay in Rome. His thoughts were quite horrific."

His face grows pale. "A temptation? Satan?"

I stifle a grin and shake my head. He understands the world as black and white. He doesn't understand there are shades of gray. There is light or the absence of light. The less light an angel carries, the darker their wings. It's hard to explain to someone like him that the true demon was the man sitting next to me. No one rivals the twisted soul of man.

"Our meeting will be brief. Please reach out to Signor La Rosa when we're done." He nods and wanders aimlessly in search of the reading glasses gripped tightly in his hand.

"Signorina De Lucio! Come sta? I thought I heard your voice. You've done something different with your hair, haven't you? Please take a seat. There is much to discuss." Cardinal Aldo Bertolucci waltzes into the meeting, followed by Sister Odette Mercier.

A smile spreads across his weathered face as he welcomes me back and points to a set of chairs by the window. I've done nothing to my hair. It's the same ponytail I wear every day, but he rarely looks at me long enough to notice.

Bertolucci is the Prefect of the Congregation for the Causes of Saints. People call it the Miracle Commission, but there's so much more to it than that. Whenever a diocese proposes a candidate for sainthood, Bertolucci and a handful of cardinals initiate years of investigation to determine if that individual is worthy.

Not just anyone becomes a saint.

The first rule is death. A candidate must be dead. There are no living saints. We then examine their lives with a fine-tooth comb. Unless they died a martyr for God, the church wants to see proof that the individual performed at least two miracles that cannot be explained through science. We consult physicians. We hire specialists and leave no stone unturned.

There are three full months left in the year, and over fifty proposals have been submitted since January. Each one merits a rigorous investigation.

The first stage is pronouncing them *Servants of God*. Everyone submitted gets that stamp. Most will make the second stage when the Pope venerates them as a person of notable regard in a special ceremony. Fewer will become Blessed or Beatified. This means the church is certain that their soul passed on to Heaven. Fewer still will be canonized as a Holy Saint of the Roman Catholic Church. The final process takes years.

I step into the process after veneration. I investigate the

validity of miracles. With less than a year on the job, I've personally investigated nine candidates. Only one passed on to beatification.

It's serious business to the Roman Curia. *And to me.*

This wasn't what I planned to do for a living, but it's a worthy task. Some nominees have been dead for centuries and some only for years. Evidence is sometimes scarce, but that doesn't make the person's contribution less important.

Like I said, we leave no stone unturned. With the help of a small team, I pore through documents, read letters, and help investigators uncover if an eyewitness to the supposed miracles is embellishing the truth. Cardinal Bertolucci's team knows what I do and believe that I see what I see.

Until I came here, I never realized what that means. *To be believed.*

I didn't offer my services. For obvious reasons, it's not something I share. Most people wouldn't understand, and if they did, they'd seek to exploit it. Bertolucci came to me.

Shortly after college graduation, he recruited me on the word of Sister Odette. She's known my family since before I was born, and although previously skeptical, she is familiar with our special gifts.

The truth is, I'm uncertain how I feel about modern-day saints, but I need to make a living. And I need to look at myself in the mirror, knowing I haven't compromised my values. This line of work affords me both.

But I wouldn't call it easy. This job takes up every waking hour and one hundred percent of my leisure time. I don't have fun. There never seems to be any time. On my last visit, I stayed for four weeks but spent most of my time traveling to a remote village in the French Alps, Budapest and the Hungarian countryside.

This time, Cardinal Lunetta insisted on purchasing me an open-ended ticket. There's no telling how long I'm expected to stay. I can only dream I'll be home by Christmas.

"Your Eminence, you mentioned something about England on the phone. Is this about the Abbott in Yorkshire?" I take out my small tablet and scribble an outline into my note-taker app.

He nods and hands me a folder. "Father Ambrose Moore died twenty years ago. A Benedictine. *You know how they can be.* Two abbeys, one in York and one in Ireland, have produced witnesses. They've petitioned His Holiness for consideration on expediting the matter. That will not happen, but we need to make it look like we're taking their request seriously."

I take the folder and grimace. "I opposed his veneration. There's something about him that doesn't sit right."

He clasps his hands and then makes the sign of the cross. "I agree with you, Livia. I got the same impression when I read his letters."

Cardinal Lunetta rolls his eyes and huffs. "You did not. You're only saying that because she got a grim feeling. You have no gifts."

Bertolucci raises his right fist in the air with righteous indignation. "The Lord filled me with the Holy Spirit and I'm telling you, I had a bad feeling. If I say I had a bad feeling, then I had a bad feeling."

Compelled to break it up before someone lunges, I ask another question. "When are we headed to Connemara?"

"The new investigator arrives tomorrow morning. He'll escort you and Sister Odette. The sisters will feel more comfortable speaking with one of their own. Ciro and I will join you in York. I believe the clergy there have been disingenuous and may have looser lips in the presence of two Cardinals."

"That suits me fine. If you'll excuse me, I need to find Inspector La Rosa. It's urgent." I stand and head for my bags. The longer I wait, the more this ominous feeling consumes me. If my delay results in someone's death, I'll never forgive myself.

"Is there something wrong?" Sister Odette follows me out. Marching across the marble floors, she struggles to keep up as I hand her my note and head for the Office of the Gendarmerie.

"That man is a hunter. I need La Rosa to alert the Polizia di Stato before it's too late." I slide across a hallway and rush down a flight of stairs. Clutching the note, the sister breaks into a sprint and urges me to take a shortcut.

Lionel Clemson's murderous intentions aren't overly concerning for me. I can take care of myself. Stepping into someone's mind allows you to control their actions. Confusion works wonders when someone follows you home and tries to force their way into your apartment. I could never harm another person. And I won't be tempted to take another person's life, even in self-defense. But I'm not above leaving someone in a state of catatonia until the police arrive.

Right now, I worry for others. That sick twerp could be out on the streets suckering some lonely American tourist into his web. Having written Lionel's full name, description and plan of action, I hand a note to La Rosa. We exchange words and I embellish a few details, unable to tell him the truth. How do you admit you read someone's mind? *It doesn't matter.* He knows I know things others don't and for that reason alone, I know he'll take it seriously.

He thanks me and rushes away to call the state police.

Weaving through a crowd of tourists, I follow a colorfully clad Swiss guard out the door and stroll towards a waiting car. I've been awake for twenty-four hours. I need to eat. I need to sleep. Tomorrow, I meet the new investigator and make the most of my only day in Rome. There won't be time for sightseeing, but I'd love a pleasant meal before I head north. It might be the only fun I have all week.

6

LUCIFER

I STEP ONTO AN ANCIENT BRIDGE AND SPOT AMON SITTING PERCHED on the stone wall that surrounds Saint Angelo's Castle. With his wings tucked in place, his gaze remains fixed on a diminutive figure in the distance. I follow his eyes and spot the girl in question. I could spot her a mile away.

"The girl in the navy-blue coat." He needlessly points to the only woman on the bridge. She's not what I expect. Someone with her abilities should have a tint of darkness. Power leads to corruption. The weakness of mortals and their hunger for power is as certain as the sun setting in the west. But not her. She's bathed in the blinding light of archangels. I've never seen anything like it.

"Do you see the man ten steps behind her? Yellow hair. Glasses. Tan trench coat. I spotted him ducked in an alleyway, watching her eat lunch through a window. He's the same man who sat next to her on the plane. I thought he reconsidered, but he must have been tailing her all along." He spreads his wings and leaps off the ledge.

Swooping past the Tiber, we hover close as she hops off the cobblestone path into a crosswalk. She knows she's being followed, but she's too preoccupied with the man behind her to spot the two buzzards flying nearby.

I study her face. There's strength in her features. Anger quashes her fears. Her eyes dart from side to side, searching for the closest police, but when none appear, she curls her fists and picks up her pace.

With every step, her neat ponytail bounces and sways from side to side in the wind. Her clenched jaw ticks until her cheekbones flush and her pale blue eyes narrow with fury.

There's no doubt she can read her stalker's mind, but can she read mine? Does she know we're here? When she turns a corner, I get my answer. Annoyed by our presence, she bats the air as if she's shooing a gnat and sends a harsh gust of wind in our path. We veer off course, too stunned to take cover.

"Was that?" Amon's eyes widen as he sways onto the street.

I nod. That's never happened. Not from a mortal. Not to me. "Go that way, I'll follow behind him."

Whizzing through camera-carrying tourists and children buzzing near a *gelateria*, she zips into a side street while she fumbles through her purse for her keys. While the man gains, he fearlessly reaches for the knife inside his coat. The sun is out. Witnesses are everywhere. But he's made it his mission to start his rampage with her. And nothing will make him deviate from his plan.

Holding her keys through her fingers like makeshift brass knuckles, she storms into a dead end and whips around to face the madman head on. I swoop out of the way, and hover overhead. In a momentarily lapse, her soft blue eyes meet mine and a beam of wondrous light short-circuits my heart. A surge of visceral longing drowns my senses and pushes me closer to the scene. I know she sees me, but she won't waste a moment acknowledging my presence.

This little girl is fierce. Her courage arouses me as much as the flash of skin peeking through her white silk blouse. Mortal women bore me. *But not her.* Something in her spirit makes my hackles rise with a primal need to protect her from harm. But I can't. The thought is ludicrous. Angels don't render aid. It's forbidden.

Frustrated and furious, I watch from above. Unable to help her or even hinder her assailant, I gaze mesmerized at the most beautiful woman I've ever seen. Her blue eyes widen as her pupils broaden with adrenaline. Her soft pink mouth curves up as she bares her teeth in a growl that makes my heart ram into my sternum.

What am I thinking?

I push the thought out of my head and wait for the dance to begin. But it's not that simple. With every tap of her patent-leather pumps, my stomach twists with a fear I've never known. If he kills her in front of me, I'll exact a quick and torturous revenge. I'll tear him from limb to limb and toss him into the watery grave he plans for her.

But what will it matter?

If he succeeds, she'll disappear. With that much light, her soul will reach paradise before I have time to finish him. She won't be reborn. She'll spend eternity with her maker in a world far beyond my reach. And I'll never set eyes on her again.

"Thought you were too good for me?" With his knife drawn, he lunges and misses.

She leaps out of the way and kicks him in the back. It's an excellent hit, but he's got a full foot and a hundred pounds on her. She's no match for his strength.

"I don't want to hurt you, but I will." She jumps back and saves herself from his swinging arm. Winding her purse strap around her forearm, she flings the heavy sack against his head, knocking him towards the wall and smashing his forehead on a protruding brick.

By the looks of his stunned expression and genuine shock when he wipes his bloody head, he wasn't expecting her to put up such a fight. But he won't give his fear away. And he won't give up on his prey.

With crazed eyes, he chuckles and licks the blood off his fingers, hoping to scare her with his lunacy. "This is happening, bitch. We do this now or I'll violate your corpse. Makes no difference to me." He crudely grabs his crotch and clumsily unzips his pants.

The sight of his erect member makes her panic. Without thinking, she shields her eyes and backs herself into a wall, gifting him the upper hand. Realizing her mistake, she scrambles to get away, but it's too late. Fueled by her rising fear, he yanks her wrist and raises his knife to strike. With her heart in his path, I SEE FUCKING RED.

I don't wait. I won't watch. Not this. *Not her.*

Before his hand comes down, I snap his neck, severing it from his spine and pull his beating heart from his chest.

Fuck him. Fuck the rules and damn the consequences.

This little girl is MINE.

7
LIVIA

Pitch black wings sweep past my head and pounce on Lionel. He has no time to scream. Darkness falls between us and I lose all sight of him in the haze. When a gust of wind shakes me off balance, I scurry backwards, and seek the wall for purchase.

I can't move. I can't scream. I'm terrorized into sudden paralysis when his giant wingspan stretches open and grazes both walls.

It's over as soon as it begins.

The crunch of bones wakes me out of my daze and makes me cower into a corner. Confused and horrified, I hold my hands to my ears and cringe as a deafening growl makes my hair stand on end. I want to look, but I can't. Trembling with primal fear, I slide to the street and brace myself for an attack.

Black wings. Not an ounce of light. *Is it him?* Has the devil come to finish the job?

While I pray, I peek through my fingers. It's a mistake. With my heart in my throat, I watch the angel punch Lionel's sternum and pull his heart clear out of his chest. Blood spatters across my face. The panic I'd fought to suppress curls its way into my heart and I fly to my feet. Adrenaline fuels my flight. Rushing down the street, I skid to a stammering halt when a second dark angel touches down and blocks my retreat. With clenched fists at his sides, he stands between me and the only exit.

"What's happening?" I fall to the ground and squeeze my eyes shut, too terrified to act. I should stop this, but I can't remember how.

The sound of fluttering wings comes closer and palpable dread consumes me. Fearing the end, I shrink as low as I can go.

"Please..." My shivering voice is so faint, it's hardly audible to me.

Silence follows footsteps. Warmth drifts into my face and my breath mingles with his. My eyes helplessly flutter open. Only inches away, a pair of steel-gray eyes meet mine and there's an instant recognition. *It's him.* A face I've seen a thousand times steals what little breath I have left.

"Please..." I whimper, still terrified by his looming presence. In the strange act of a madwoman, I reach for my purse and hold it between us. Hot tears stream down my face.

Ominous and intense, he tilts his head and sniffs the surrounding air. "You can see me? You can really see me?" His deep voice floats through the air like chords from an untuned piano. Jarring and painful. For no reason, a smile touches his lips and the darkness he carries glows brighter with a spark of light.

"We'll meet again, Livia." He lifts a lone finger in the air and gently taps my forehead.

The world goes black.

8

LUCIFER

THIS DOESN'T HAPPEN TO ME. MY HEART IS A BROKEN, BARREN wasteland. Nothing gets in. Nothing grows. Since my expulsion, there's been no room for anyone but me.
Until now.
Livia intrigues me. The light in her beckons the light that once shone just as bright inside me. Ever since I laid eyes on her, I've felt utterly infatuated and driven by an unfamiliar madness.
I terrified her. I regret it. Perhaps my rage got the best of me. But he had it coming, and I don't regret ending his wretched life. When it was done, I wiped the memory from her mind and carried her limp body home.
The size of her apartment surprised me. It's a humble space for someone who works for the Holy See. I know she can afford more but she doesn't seem to covet extravagance. Her place is nothing more than a bed, bureau, and desk. No television or stereo. I respect that but I want to give her more. I like her. I don't know why, but my heart clamors for hers. This is the strangest thing I've ever felt.
When she finally awakened, I kept my distance. Not

completely. I watched her from the roof of a building on the other side of the street. She ate dinner alone, prayed for much too long and read a book about how to care for dogs. Her innocence is as remarkable as it is refreshing.

I can't believe she could see me. I hid my appearance and she still saw me as clear as day. There was no doubt about it. She looked straight into my eyes and spoke to me in my mind. I wish I could tell her who I am, but that's too risky. As much as I want to soothe her fears, she won't seek solace in my arms.

So why am I dressed in my best suit and posing as a paranormal investigator for the Miracle Commission? This is the only way. I don't want to deceive her, but she won't let me in if she knows who I am. No one wants to fall in love with Lucifer.

With impeccably forged credentials, I breeze through Vatican security and march up a lengthy flight of stairs littered with tourists. I despise this place, and not for the obvious reasons. My skin won't burn off in holy places, but everything about this ostentatious shrine turns my stomach.

Across town, children go hungry, but here clergy strut by me draped in gold crosses and designer cassocks. It's a despicable display of vanity and wealth. Nothing would thrill me more than to get my hands on these red-clad cardinals and toss them all into the deepest waters of the Tyrrhenian Sea. It would be my finest work.

As I walk down the long hallway towards Cardinal Bertolucci's office, my heavy footfalls echo off the marble floor, drawing attention from every room I pass. My entrance sounds as ominous as it feels. When I reach my destination, I hold my breath and stare vacantly at the enormous mahogany door.

Panic grips me. What if she remembers my face? She has a sight I don't understand. This might be unintentionally cruel. The last thing I want to do is frighten her before I explain my intentions. But what are my intentions? *Fuck, I don't know.* Flustered, I turn to leave, but it's too late.

The heavy door swings open.

"Signor Angeli? They told me you were on your way. Please come in." A pinched face nun in a simple black dress and sensible shoes welcomes me into the cardinal's ornate office. There is no one else here.

"*Buongiorno*, my name is Sister Odette Mercier. I'll accompany you and Signorina De Lucio to Connemara tomorrow morning. Please make yourself comfortable. Cardinal Bertolucci is on his way. Sit wherever you like." She makes a gesture, nudging me further into the room and points to a group of leather captain's chairs.

"*Buongiorno. Grazie.*" I take a chair and watch her thumb through a stack of papers pertaining to the case at hand, Father Ambrose Moore. I knew him well. Too well for a man of the cloth. His death brought me days of immense glee. I can't believe that miscreant is being considered for sainthood. The mere thought is outrageous.

"We have new witnesses?" I pry. I know we do, but I want to gauge her feelings.

She nods but shows no outward emotion. "Two Benedictine sisters claim to have information. We'll be interviewing them before we meet His Eminence in Yorkshire. They have divulged nothing more than that. We'll know more when we arrive. The signorina always uncovers the truth." Sister Odette is a blank slate. No guile or ulterior motives. She's careful with her words, but not duplicitous.

"Will she be here today?" I make conversation to pass the time. I know she's in the building.

"Yes, she and I arrived together earlier this morning for our morning prayers." She clasps her hands and nods.

Morning prayers? She prayed for over an hour last night. That sounds excessive. First thing I'm doing is making her live a little.

"That poor girl works herself to the bone. She and the cardinal had an audience with His Holiness, and I believe they're finishing their breakfast now. Can I call for some tea or coffee? It shouldn't be much long..." Her words cut off. "Oh, I think I hear them coming."

The cardinal walks in first, and I jump to my feet to greet him. Oblivious to my identity, his smile broadens as he approaches. Most holy rollers think they can sense the presence of darkness, but they're full of it. I passed dozens of priests on my way here. No one flinched.

"Signor Angeli? It's a pleasure." He too is an open book. His mind jumps from one thought to another, but everything concerns the business of his office. He's worried about Father Moore. He believes he's unworthy, and he's counting on Livia to uncover something in Ireland. He doesn't appear to have an agenda. I'm genuinely surprised.

"Thank you, Your Eminence. I'm grateful for the opportunity." We shake hands and he turns to look at the door. "Signorina, where are you?"

"Forgive me. Cardinal Lunetta wanted a word." She floats in with downcast eyes. "Is the investigator..." Surprise makes her speech falter. As her gaze drifts to mine, a flicker of recognition simmers in her crystal blue irises. I fear she knows who I am.

"Signorina, this is Signor Angeli. Luca Angeli. He comes highly recommended." Bertolucci pauses and turns to me. "Signore, this is Livia De Lucio. She is indisputably our most valuable collaborator."

"Please, call me Luca." I extend my hand and she trembles slightly as she shakes the tip of my fingers. When she pulls away, a tiny spark lingers in my hand, like a fizzling current. I'm not sure if it came from her or me, but a sudden sense of abandonment tears through my heart.

"It's a pleasure, Signor Angeli." A tiny smile forms and disappears before her mind goes black. All thoughts, words and images disappear behind a thick curtain that shuts me out.

I nod and try harder to break through. It's impenetrable. "Yes. May I call you Livia?"

"Of course." Her brows crease with concern, but she forces a smile and continues.

"I've made you a copy of my notes from preliminary interviews. We can discuss it on the flight tomorrow after you've caught up. They booked sister Odette and me on the 8:00am Alitalia flight leaving from Ciampino Airport. We reserved your spot. Please confirm your passport information with the travel office after the meeting." She brushes past me and gracefully falls into the chair across from the cardinal.

Throughout this mind-numbing conversation, she avoids my glare. I have no access to her thoughts but detect no outward signs of fear. On the contrary, she carries an air of serenity that soothes me as she speaks. My hackles calm. Years of bitterness and aggravation strangely disintegrate as I watch the movement of her lips and the soft sway of her hands. I wish I knew what she was thinking.

I don't know much about women. I rarely observe them in the wild. There was never a need to examine their features. I learn what I need to play my part. The only emotions I've ever felt in their presence are apathy, anger, and the occasional pity. Once I witness their temptation or trial, I'm done. But it's impossible to pretend I'm not ferociously aroused.

Her eyes suddenly dart to mine. She can read my mind. My identity is out of her reach, but I want her to know why I'm here. I'm here for her.

Luca Angeli is here for her.

She'll meet Lucifer later.

Rattled by the devious thoughts ruminating in my lust-addled brain, she pulls the long dark waves off her face and hoists her silky locks into a messy bun. She fidgets and smooths her hair to keep her hands busy.

Her smart suit, black and conservative, sits over a powder blue high-collared blouse that matches her kind blue eyes. She might be tiny in stature, but she commands everyone's attention with her confidence and expertise. With all his experience and tenure, the cardinal continuously looks to her for guidance. But her modesty never wavers.

"Signor Angeli, are you certain you're prepared to join us in Ireland?" She finally addresses me directly, but I'm too lost in admiration to hear the question.

"Pardon?" A few rapid blinks to focus and my eyes lock on hers. An unfamiliar yearning takes hold of my heart and fills my mind with thoughts no angel should entertain. For the first time, I'm relieved I'm beyond redemption. Those rules don't apply to me.

"Perhaps it would be best if you joined us in Yorkshire. That allows you time to catch up on the interviews." She stares thoughtfully and waits for my answer.

She wants to ditch me. *I don't think so.*

I run my hand down my cheek and massage my clenched jaw. "I've done my own research. I have a hunch the sisters do not have pleasant news to share." I'm not sure what possesses me to say so much, but words tumble out before I can stop them.

She quirks a quizzical brow. "You sound certain."

I nod and stop to memorize each button on her blouse, wondering if they'd be difficult to unravel. "I am. As I said, I've done my research."

She stands to gather her things, shrugging her jacket tighter around her full breasts, keenly aware of my wandering eyes. "Suit yourself, Signor Angeli. We will see you in Galway tomorrow."

Slightly out of breath, she turns to Sister Odette. "Sister, I'll see you bright and early for our prayers. We need all the help we can get this coming week."

She gives me her hand. "Luca, it was a pleasure. I look forward to working with you. If you'll excuse me, I have a meeting and need to confirm arrangements for England." With a polite nod, she scurries out of the room.

I jump to my feet and follow her out. "Livia?" I catch up and slide beside her in the hallway.

Her eyes grow wide, but she keeps walking. "Yes? Do you have a question?"

"I do. Will you have dinner with me... tonight?" I can't believe my ears. I'm asking a woman out on a date. But this is what men do. Isn't it? Isn't this how they make women love them? If they can do it, so can I.

She scuffs the floor as she skids to a hard stop. "Excuse me? Signore, this is the Vatican, not a nightclub. Your offer is incredibly inappropriate." She winces at the volume of her voice and covers her beautiful, plump lips with her hand.

My confidence flees. "Forgive me. I meant to preface my proposal. I mean a working dinner. I'd like to discuss tomorrow's interviews in greater detail, if you're available. Moore does not deserve to be canonized. I believe I can help you discover what you need." I stutter like a schoolboy and try to ignore the sound of my thundering heart.

Her trembling fingers tighten a button that's firmly in place. "A work dinner? With you?" For a moment, her mind bursts open. She's too flustered to control the thoughts racing through her head as she tries to summon the strength to run for the hills.

"I don't bite. I know you're used to working alone but we'll be working together for the foreseeable future. It's not unusual to share meals with co-workers. Is it?" I stop at the bottom of the stairs and turn to face her. "I'll meet you wherever you like, and I won't keep you out late. Tomorrow will be difficult. You need your rest."

She clutches her bag to her body as she searches the landscape for a thoughtful way to turn me down. "I don't usually..."

I interrupt her. "How about 6:30? There's nothing wicked about a 6:30 dinner."

She nods demurely and brushes a loose strand of hair off her flushed face. "There's a place on Via dei Coronari called Pietro's. I'll meet you there at 6:30... for a work dinner." She runs off like a frightened cat and I watch her until she disappears into another office.

The moment she leaves my sight, my heart aches to see her again. I've never felt anything like this before. Is this love? It feels like I'm slipping into the realm of insanity.

Why would anyone do this on purpose?

9
LIVIA

This is a test. I can feel it.

One day after I witness a temptation, a swarthy Italian with the most masculine sinewy hands I've ever seen walks into my life. Tall, dark, undeniably fit and unspeakably handsome, Signor Angeli is no ordinary man.

And this is no ordinary test.

The Devil must know the darkest secrets of my heart. It's no coincidence my guardian angel has fled. For the first time since infancy, I'm alone and left entirely to my own defenses. The Almighty has thrown me to the wolves and the alpha is sharpening his teeth.

I draw a shaky breath into my lungs and silently pray for strength.

I have no business sharing a meal with him. I should have said no. I could have stood him up. Every step here felt like I was walking into a trap. But I couldn't stop myself from coming. His animal magnetism weakened my steel resolve and my fluttering heart led the way.

"Do you have something on your mind? You haven't said a

word since they brought the food." He lifts his chiseled chin, narrowing his eyes as he gauges my expression.

Our eyes meet and I once again try to read his thoughts. *Nothing.* He's blocked me out. How did he do that? Angeli... Does he come from angels? *Is he like me?*

Maybe this is for the best. After this afternoon's play-by-play of my impending seduction, I don't think I'm ready to see more.

"Forgive my rudeness. I'm worried about tomorrow." I take a small bite, fiddle with my napkin, and return to Luca's penetrating stare. My stomach flops. I'm not accustomed to being around men and it's hard to concentrate in the company of such flawlessly beautiful lips.

What am I saying? This is unlike me. I'm sensible. Devout. Impervious to charm. This man is in league with demons. *He must be.* One smile and few bats of his ridiculously long lashes and I've unraveled into a harlot. Do I need an exorcism? Do those things work when they're not actually inhabiting your body?

Not yet, anyway.

Good heavens. Where's my mind?

He raises a perfectly manscaped eyebrow. "Tomorrow?"

"The Irish nuns. I fear their revelations will place the cardinal at odds with the Roman Curia. Do you mean what you said about Father Moore? You share my suspicions?" I swallow hard, fearful he'll hear the anxiety in my voice. It's easier to discuss work. The more we dive into the Sisters, the sooner this fire simmering in my belly will fizzle out.

He nods and takes a bite of gnocchi. "I do. He was a degenerate. And his soul has not passed onto heaven. You can see as well as me. Can't you?" He licks his full lips and tilts his gorgeous head as he waits for my reply. This temptation feels exceptionally cruel. Ruthless, perhaps. What have I done that merits this?

No, it's not my place to ask. That's presumptuous. There must be a greater plan at work, and I have no cause to question it. *Stay strong, Livia.* Don't turn into those women who fall for the first hot man who propositions her. Who cares if he's handsome? *Beautiful.* All right, maybe, breathtaking. He's here to offer a fool's paradise. This is far too good to be true.

"I can't say for sure. How do you know what I see?" I flash my eyes to his then look away. My stomach twists in knots as butterflies swirl and crash, blinded by my exploding lust.

He smiles, then stumbles on his words. "I just… know. You and I are not so different." Electricity crackles and lingers on the inflection of his sultry voice. In a moment of imprudent desire, my lonely heart floats into his hands, eager to be consumed.

Please get a hold of yourself. He's reeling you in like a dead fish.

I clasp my hands in my lap and bite down on my bottom lip. "I thought I was alone. Since my family passed, I've never met anyone… like me." My cheeks catch fire.

A smile spreads across his face. "I've waited ages to find someone like you. You'll never be alone again."

I cover my heart with my hand. If I didn't know what I know and see what I see, those sexy words might send me flying into his lap. But I need to be cautious. This could be the answer to a lifetime of prayers or send me straight into damnation. "I fear this conversation has gone off the rails. I'm here because you said you'd help."

He interrupts. "Forgive me. I promise, I mean no disrespect. Perhaps, I enjoy your company too much." His words soften, but his hungry gaze sharpens and spears my flailing heart.

Struggling in vain to keep my pulse in check. "Forgive my rudeness. I appreciate any help you can provide."

He sips his wine and lays his hand over mine. "I understand you doubt me. You don't know me…yet. You will."

I quietly sigh and run my fingers down my mother's crucifix. The longer I remain in his presence, the weaker I become.

"What do you do for fun, Livia?" His eyes sparkle.

"Stuff. Why?" I raise an eyebrow.

"I'm curious. You're young and it's obvious this work weighs heavy on your soul. What do you do for fun?" He pours himself another glass of wine and offers me more.

I hold my hand over the rim. "No, thank you. I've had enough. I work. I attend Mass. I read. There isn't much time for anything else."

He raises his hand to ask for the check. "Let's change that. Take a walk with me and tell me your life story over gelato."

"It's too chilly for gelato." I shake my head and button my cardigan, anxiously aware of his focus.

"Nonsense. I'll keep you warm."

10

LUCIFER

W<small>HAT AM</small> I <small>DOING</small>?

I'm wearing cologne. I bought a new suit. I spent twenty fucking minutes fixing my hair. I'm flirting like a two-bit hustler and if I get any harder, this table will flip over on its side.

I owe humans a formal apology. For seven thousand years, I've shown little sympathy for your struggles. I believed your choice was simple. I couldn't have been more wrong. Some choices are beyond control.

I've tempted billions, but I've never been tempted like this. No one has offered me anything I wanted. No one has dangled a poisoned fruit that rendered the fulfillment of my heart's desire while simultaneously cursing me to a life of torment.

Nothing moved me. Nothing appealed to my basest instincts. I never fully understood the power of lust born from love until Livia De Lucio walked into Pietro's sporting a tight black dress and a plunging neckline that's kept me on the edge of my seat, salivating to glimpse an inch of supple cleavage. It's been centuries since I've been with a woman, and my only motivation was curiosity. I never yearned to feel her skin on mine, my lips on hers or our bodies melded together in the throes of passion.

This is different. I want all of that and more.

Every time her baby blue eyes wander to mine, the beat of my heart soars to such dizzying heights I fear it will sprout wings and leave me for good. With every glance, my affection deepens, and my senses drown with desire. Every word she whispers, elevates my senses and leaves me thirsting for more. I've just eaten my first meal in decades and yet a powerful hunger twists my belly into knots I have no strength to untangle.

No one's ever looked at me the way Livia does. No one smiles at me. *This is a first.* Every time her full pink lips curve into a smile meant for me and me only, I want to fly across the table and give her a thousand reasons to save each one for me.

While I pay the check, I shift in my seat to give the cock tenting these trousers room to breathe. I wish I knew what she was thinking. Does she know who I am? Is she toying with me?

When I look up, Livia's curious gaze greets mine. Shying away, she peeks at me from under a pair of fluttering lashes. She's exquisite and entirely unaware of it. "Thank you for treating me. I'll buy your dinner in Galway tomorrow night. If we can manage it."

Choking back emotions I've never felt, I nod and offer her a pathetic smile. "We'll manage it. After all, we have to eat."

She bobs her head in a nervous nod and shrinks in her seat. Craving her touch, I stand to help her up. When I offer my arm, she doesn't hesitate to take it. The look of trust in her eyes slays me.

With her arm entwined in mine, we step out onto the cobblestone path and walk side by side on a narrow sidewalk. As a passing couple approaches, I bring her tighter into my embrace to make room for them. She stiffens momentarily, then relaxes against my ribs, nuzzling her cheek on my jacket. My heart races as I breathe the soft scent of her perfume and bask in the warm glow of her light.

While we walk and talk, I spot her cowardly guardian perched on a nearby roof. He fears me too much to come closer, but his frantic expression assures me he's called for support. My arm winds tighter around her waist as a sinking feeling takes hold of my senses. I don't know what I'll do if they don't let me keep her. This is only the beginning, and I can't imagine spending eternity without her.

No matter where this takes us or where we end up, I need us to go together.

I've never needed anyone or anything. *But I need Livia.*

11

LIVIA

"How long have you seen angels?" His words surprise me. I didn't expect to discuss something like this so soon.

"Who said I do?" While I search my mind for an answer that might satisfy his question, I lick the pistachio gelato sliding down my oversized cone. I don't enjoy being dishonest, but I don't want to give too much away. People's opinions change, and typically not for the better. I'm not sure how I feel about Luca, but I know I don't want him to think I'm crazy.

Mumbling through his cold dessert, he clarifies. "I told you we're not so different." His charm falters as he stammers and stumbles over a protruding cobblestone. I don't understand this man. One second, he's charismatic and sexy and the next he's a bumbling teenage boy too nervous to look me in the eye. If I wasn't certain he had ulterior motives, I'd almost find it endearing.

He gestures for me to walk ahead as we pass a long line of tourists. "You don't have to tell me. But I'd like to know more about you."

While we amble through the crowded piazza, his dark restless gaze dips to me and I lose the ability to form words. Maybe this isn't a temptation. Maybe this is fate. He could be the man I always knew would find me. What are the chances? It's not impossible. Is it?

I take a slow lick off my soggy cone and meet his hungry gaze. "It runs in my family. My father's side claimed we come from angels. From the Nephilim. Perhaps that's just a clever explanation. I just know I see things I shouldn't."

His lips curve into a tender smile before he shoves a generous helping of chocolate gelato between his plump lips. "Do you believe in fate, Livia?"

I avoid the question. This is getting out of hand. I've flirted shamelessly with a handsome co-worker. I'm just as guilty as him. If we stay on course, things will move to the next level. Although, I'm not entirely clear what that level entails.

This is a tough week. Chances are high we'll spend every waking moment with one another. That has trouble written all over it. And I don't like trouble. I've lusted in my heart and that's as far as this will go.

"Thank you for dinner. My place is up ahead. Are we giving you a lift to the airport?" I'm out of my element and easy prey for someone this slick. The best thing to do is flee before things get out of hand.

He shakes his head. "I've got an earlier flight. I'll meet you in Ireland, Miss De Lucio." He lifts my hand to his lips and kisses my knuckles. Heat pulses between my legs. This is unprecedented... and flagrant. I'm such an amateur, this man will eat me alive.

"Until tomorrow." I stutter a pathetic goodbye while I stare at the sidewalk, avoiding the sexiest eyes in creation.

"Tomorrow can't come soon enough." He winks and leads me towards the front of my building.

Galled by this brazen flirtation, I open my mouth to end these shenanigans, but a swarm of butterflies seizes my heart. Struggling to utter a few words of disapproval, I squeak out what I can. "It's best if we keep this... professional."

"Forgive me." His gaze cruises the length of my body before his eyes return to mine. "You're unbelievably beautiful. I'm not myself around you." His velvet tenor sends treacherous shivers down my spine. I can't stay in his company one second more.

"Signor Angeli, you're very kind. I appreciate the compliment... but..." My head dizzies as every word stabs my aching heart. Why did they hire such a handsome investigator?

"But what? You don't find me attractive? I don't believe you." He smiles, wraps a powerful arm around my waist and slams me into his chest. My waffle cone and mouth fall to the floor.

His nerve.

His pompous audacity.

That damn cologne.

I've had enough.

I push my hands into his heavenly chest and attempt to squirm out of his grip. How can I want him? He's a stranger. This is lunacy. I'm a twenty-three-year-old virgin with years of experience brushing men off. How did he break through so quickly?

"You forget yourself."

He shakes his head and pulls me into my building. With my back against the wall and his mouth inches from mine, my heart threatens to beat right out of my chest. "I know. I've forgotten everything, Livia. And I don't want to remember."

My heart melts and my eyes mist. I'm crumbling too fast. "I know what you're doing."

He presses his forehead to mine and closes his eyes. "What am I doing? Please tell me, because I don't think I know."

"Everyone has a choice. Everyone makes choices to be good or bad..." My trembling voice sputters as his eyes hold me hostage.

"No." He cuts me off.

My lips part in confusion. "Pardon?"

"No. This doesn't feel like a choice. Does it? Somethings are meant to be. You and I are meant to be." His words trail off as his head tilts and his lips crash into mine. With a fiery kiss that renders me boneless, he devours my lips and brings my body to life. With every swipe of his tongue, he steals my breath and demands my surrender. His warmth, his scent, the feel of his hands gliding down my body brings my latent sexuality to a raging boil.

"Luca..." I whimper against his mouth, trying desperately to salvage my modesty, but no meaningful words come to mind. I can't go further, but I have no strength to push him away. I can't take him upstairs, but I don't want him to stop.

"Livia..." His kisses turn gentle as he pulls away and cups my face with his giant hands. "Could you fall in love with me?"

A sudden and indescribable sadness grips my heart. Something's wrong. All I want to do is sink into his warm embrace, but something makes me pull away. This feels tragically flawed. Whatever we are, whatever we could be, can't go further than this. Shaking my head, I gaze into his dark eyes and breathe the only words my mouth will form.

"I'll see you in Ireland. Goodnight."

12
LUCIFER

THIS DEAFENING SILENCE PLAGUES ME. TWO DAYS AGO, I PREVENTED Livia's death. I don't know if I changed her fate. There's a high probability she was meant to survive all along. She's a powerful girl with abilities I've never encountered in another human, but I couldn't take that chance. I couldn't stand idly by and let someone hurt her.

My interference will have consequences. Surely, I forfeited any chance of redemption. But that's not my concern. The only thing that matters is Livia.

"Of course, they know." Samael stokes the fire kindling in the drawing room of a small inn in Galway. Posing as a departing guest, he sips a cup of breakfast tea and slides into an oversized chair. His green cable-knit sweater makes him blend in with the locals, but it's not what I'd expect from the Angel of Death.

"That is *some* jumper." I lean back into the soft leather couch and cross my ankle to my knee.

He grimaces. "It's October. This is Ireland." He points out the window and adjusts his sleeves. "It's fucking cold. You know how much I hate to be cold."

"There's no doubt they know everything. That's not what I asked. Why hasn't anyone come to me with a list of grievances? Why haven't they threatened? Ever since I saved her, I've been waiting for the other shoe to drop." I run my hand through my hair and sigh with frustration. I can't get her out of my head. Every time I close my eyes, memories of last night drown me in waves of restless lust. Patience is a virtue. And no one's ever accused me of being virtuous.

She thinks she's clever. She thinks she slammed that tiny foot and put me in my place. I know my place. *It's with her.* And the sooner she lets me sweep her off her feet, the sooner we can move on to the exchange of sexual favors.

I'm really looking forward to that part.

Samael lifts his pinky as he sips his tea, careful not to spill anything on his hideous outfit. He's the only one of us who is still allowed to enter the halls of heaven. I didn't expect his visit, but I rely on him to provide information I lack. "I've kept my ear to the ground. Nothing. No one's mentioned you or Livia. It's coming. You know it is. Be prepared to argue your case."

I take a deep breath and crack my knuckles. My anger rises at breakneck speed. "Why are you here? Is there something you need? I thought you had news."

"I was in the neighborhood and thought I'd pop in to see you. Do I need a reason?" His eyes drift off. He's only physically here. His mind is somewhere else. I've heard the rumors. Samael's in love with a guardian angel. He must have stalked her to Ireland.

I stifle a grin and feign contempt. "When you get your head out of the clouds, do you think you can do some investigation? Do I need to promote Asmodeus? Why haven't you asked your little friend?"

He bristles at the suggestion. "You know I do my job. Do you have any idea how busy I am any given day? Death never stops." He folds his arms across his chest like a petulant toddler. "And leave her out of it. She's still beside herself with grief. It took weeks to get back in her good graces."

I roll my eyes conspicuously enough for him to see. "Livia is due any minute now. Instead of spending all your time hounding that guardian, can you investigate this for me? All this silence makes me anxious."

"I'm hounding? *Luca Angeli? Seriously?* What sort of disguise is that? Besides, I suspect you haven't thought this through. What are your intentions? Are you going to carry this on until her death? Unless she sins, you have no authority to toy with her destiny." He lectures as he gifts me with an image I want to forget. I don't need to be reminded of Livia's mortality. That pain weighs on my heart like a cinder block.

Samael's out of line. His unrequited infatuation makes him testy and his mood makes him bold. Although I can empathize, I won't tolerate his tone. I flick my wrist and send an invisible punch to his abdomen. He can't typically feel pain, but he can always feel mine.

The surprise makes the air leaves his lungs. Hunched over and gasping for air, he lifts his palms in remorse. Gritting his teeth, he stammers out an insincere apology. "Forgive me. I'll see what I can do."

"What?" I snap at his qualifying statement.

His upper lip curls in a defiant sneer and he nods with distinct hesitation. I rarely make demands, but when I do, I expect unwavering cooperation. "Fine. I'll ask her to speak with Livia's guardian. He must know something."

I nod and glance at my watch. "Why do you make things difficult on yourself?"

"I must be a glutton for punishment." His voice drips with sarcasm. "But in all sincerity, how long are you keeping this up?"

The sound of Livia's voice draws my attention to the door, and my heart flies out of my chest. Today will be hard. She's bound to be vulnerable. It's the perfect time to pounce. "I'll keep it up as long as it takes. Until I know she's mine. Until we marry."

"Marry?" His mouth falls open. "Are you serious?"

"Leave me. Don't return until you know more."

13

LIVIA

"My dear, are you feeling well? You've been distracted all morning." Sister Odette holds a firm hand to my forehead, then checks her own. This is unconscionable. She's got so much on her mind, and now my nasty thoughts are adding to her stress.

He kissed me. I can't believe he kissed me. *And what a kiss.* It was better than anything I ever imagined. I didn't know you could feel a kiss everywhere. But I did. When his strong but oh so soft lips fell on mine, I thought I'd die on the spot. It felt like something out of a movie. A good movie. The kind they don't show until after 10:00pm.

What must he think? He must know I liked it. The air buzzed with sexual tension. No matter how much I tried to regain control of my senses, I'd played my terrible hand and lost. I didn't want him to stop. I let him cop a few good feels before I feigned offense and ran upstairs. That beautiful man has my number. He's got it, he used it, and I know he'll use it again.

To my surprise, I hope he does.

I nod and try to hide my guilt. "It's nothing, Sister. My concern is for the day ahead. This won't be a simple interview. I received word that Bishop Dempsey, a former colleague of Bishop Moore, plans to accompany us to the abbey. We never requested his escort and I fear he may pressure them into silence."

Her expression shrinks into sadness. "That was my first impression as well. I hope we're wrong. It's exceedingly brave for these sisters to come forward. If they're pressured into silence, others will know their testimony is not sincerely coveted. His Eminence does not want to canonize an unworthy soul. We must remember that." She gives my hand a squeeze and directs my gaze to Galway Bay. The view stuns us both.

"You've never been to this side of Ireland, have you?" She smiles and points to a stretch of colorful houses lining the water.

I shake my head. "I spent a week in Dublin earlier this year. It reminded me of Northern England. This is how I imagined Ireland would look. I wish we were here under better circumstances."

She pats my lap. "You must take some time to enjoy yourself, Livia. You're a young woman. I know you want a family. You deserve a good husband who loves you. Those things won't fly out of the sky. You need to make yourself available to receive God's blessings. I'm not sure if you've noticed, but Signor Angeli is an exceptionally handsome man."

My cheeks catch fire. Oh, my Lord, she's on to me. "No, he's a co-worker. That's dangerous and inappropriate. Besides, I don't think I'm ready for such things. Work satisfies for now." I lie through my teeth.

This is disgraceful. In less than twenty-four hours, I've veered off course and jumped on the entrance ramp leading straight to hell. First, I let a strange man fondle me in a darkened hallway and now I've lied to a nun.

"My dear, it will happen when it happens. Don't run from your fate because you fear a loss of control. Guard your heart but don't lock it away." She studies the landscape as she speaks, closing her eyes every few minutes to ponder something she won't share. She often speaks of Ireland, but never elaborates on reasons why she holds it close to her heart. I won't intrude on her thoughts. If her memories are too precious to share, I'll let her keep them all to herself.

"Livia, where did you find this inn? It's absolutely charming." She leans towards my window and we gaze side by side at the 18th century home that was recently converted into a cozy bed-and-breakfast. I'm glad she likes it. This week will be gruesome, and I want her to have a comfortable room to recuperate from the ugliness of the day.

"It had the best ratings. Apart from a woman who disliked their curtain patterns, it had the most *Superbs* on the travel website I trust most." I step out onto the street and follow the driver to the back of the car. Obviously Catholic, he almost curtsies to Sister Odette as he carefully hands each of our bags to the bellman. She wants to laugh but assures him she'll pray for him and his family at the earliest convenience.

With a tip of his hat, he bids us good day and waits for us to follow the perfectly lined path towards the door. This isn't unusual. One look at a nun's habit or a priest's cassock and people humbly submit with sycophantic deference. Things only get worse when we're in the company of the cardinals.

As I follow Sister Odette through the brightly painted door, my eyes drift from side to side, scanning the room for any signs of Luca. In minutes, my façade of indifference collapses.

"Ladies, I'm delighted to see you." Luca appears from the shadows and slides the heavy bags off our shoulders. He walks ahead and thankfully avoids my wistful gaze.

While he makes small talk with the man hauling our larger bags, I let my eyes stray from the back of his head to his broad shoulders and thick arms. The cut of the more casual tweed blazer he's chosen to wear highlights the curve of his corded biceps and accentuates the small waist that sits beneath his powerful back.

His mouth-watering frame is a buffet for my starved sexuality. When he finally turns and greets me with a smile, I feel I may faint.

"Are you well?" Luca extends his arm and catches my swaying body. I'm mortified. Distracted by my lusty observations, the protective wall I've built around my thoughts crumbles to the ground. If he's like me, he knows everything. The naughty dreams. The passionate musings that always end with Luca pushing an antique pram around the Orange Garden while we watch the sunset over Rome and chase the rescue Chihuahua I plan to adopt.

He must have seen it all.

"Thank you. I fear she's exhausted herself. Cardinal Bertolucci relies on her too much. Poor thing's been to six countries in the last month and there's no end in sight until the holidays." Sister Odette works herself into a tizzy while I remain cradled in Luca's arms, unsure if I should dust myself off or bask in his musky scent a few minutes more.

"Are you all right? Can you stand?" He tilts me forward but holds my hand to his chest, letting me steady myself on his massive chest. The dizziness returns.

I give him a quick, almost indiscernible nod and dig my fingers into his hard pecs, crawling up to get a firm foot on the ground. I've never been so shameless. "Thank you. I think I'm better now."

"Have you eaten? Has she eaten?" He doesn't trust me to answer the question. But he's right. I'm just about to nod when Sister Odette chimes in.

"No. She's been a ball of nerves all morning. Nothing before the flight and nothing during." She brings her finger to her lips. "Perhaps it's low blood sugar.

As much as I hate being mothered and diagnosed by people who never set foot in medical school, I need an excuse for my strange behavior. "You're probably right. We'll stop somewhere on the way to Connemara."

With a hint of mischief in his dark eyes, Luca takes my bags and makes me lead the way upstairs. When we reach the top, he makes room for Sister Odette and the inn's only bellman to head toward her room before following me to mine.

"I have a surprise for you." He whispers as he unlocks my door and gestures for me to pass through.

"A surprise?" I keep my enthusiasm in check, but his silky voice sends my pulse into the stratosphere. What could it be? Another kiss? The possibilities are endless.

After he sets my luggage down, he returns to my side and runs a finger down my nose. "You'll need to wait until this afternoon. I'm not thrilled about the way you ran off last night."

My heart races and fills with remorse. I had no choice. I was teetering too close to the edge. One more kiss would have undone twenty-three years of unsullied behavior. "I'm sorry. But I fear if things get out of hand, we'll never rein it in."

He brushes the hair off my face and stifles a crooked grin. "Good. You've been reined in long enough. It's time to set you free."

14
LUCIFER

WHAT AN UNBELIEVABLE TURN OF EVENTS. I HARDLY RECOGNIZE myself. Nothing knocks you on your ass and shreds your insides like the threat of unrequited love. But for three precious minutes, she let her guard down and let me in. It was miraculous. I saw the longing I feel every time I feast my eyes on her gorgeous, ripe body. I took a glimpse at the tame fantasies her innocent mind produces.

Sorry, sweetheart. Things are getting way raunchier than that.

The hardest part will be getting her to admit it. She has feelings she doesn't understand. She thinks we're a tragedy waiting to unfold. Perhaps we are. But we'll never know if we don't see this through.

For the first time since I landed on this godforsaken world, I have hope. This isn't a terrible place to begin. And I can't ask for more so soon. I saw the future she wants, and I want to give it to her. If I can. If they let me.

Fuck. What if they don't let me?

I don't think I could tempt her into a big enough sin to place her in a spiritually compromised position. The only thing I can guarantee is a little fornication, and since I'm actively involved, I'm fairly certain it won't be held against her. What other options do I have? She's sure as hell not fornicating with anyone else.

This is my dilemma. Her strength of character is what makes her shine so bright. I don't want to dim her light or compromise her soul. But I can't let her go. She's crawled under my skin and burrowed her way into my heart. I know that's terribly unromantic, but that's how it feels.

I've been invaded. Conquered by a pair of blue eyes and bee-stung lips. I feel no shame in my weakness for her. I never dreamed I could feel anything like this. I never deserved it. And I don't deserve Livia. If I capture her heart, I'll move heaven and earth to protect it forever.

I'll need to confess who I am. It feels risky. She's waiting for the man of her dreams. Not Satan. I've always thought highly of myself, but even I know I'm not prototypical husband material. How do I explain I've changed? For her, I can be better. For her, I'll rise from the ashes of my disgrace, knock her socks clear off her feet and conquer this wretched world in her honor.

No, that's not what I meant.

Obviously, I still need work. I won't be too hard on myself. Love is a new emotion. I'm a work in progress.

After a twenty-minute separation, I rush down the stairs, impatient to see her again. With muted hope, I scan the room for her beautiful face. She's hiding. I can smell the lingering air of her perfume, but she's nowhere in sight.

Sister Odette appears from behind. Wearing a somber expression, she clasps her hands to her waist and sighs.

"Signor Angeli, will you check on Livia? She stepped outside to speak with Bishop Dempsey. He insists on accompanying us to Kylemore, and neither of us believe that's a good idea. I just had a quick chat with His Eminence, and he agrees with us. I don't know why it's taking so long to send him away." She shakes her head and clutches her crucifix.

"I'll get rid of him." I grind my teeth and head to the door. I'm sure she can take care of herself, but someone like Dempsey, a man who's risen through the church hierarchy in record time, won't take no for an answer.

As soon as I step outside, I see Livia's exasperated expression. He's not listening to her. She's laid out a long list of reasons for him to stay behind in Galway, but he's ignored or countered each one by gaslighting her concerns. I'm on to his schemes. He wants to silence the nuns and intimidate others from coming forth. He'd love to say a bona fide saint mentored him.

By the time I reach them, he's dismissed her argument and turns to head for the hired car. This won't do. No one dismisses Livia.

"Father Dempsey?" I deliberately demote him as I swagger towards the end of the yard. His eyes flash to mine and his mouth parts to correct me. Nothing comes out. A strangled cry escapes as I hold him paralyzed to speak. When my eyes flicker red, his fat face pales. A thousand sins wash through his mind. Sins, he's forgotten. Memories that haunt him. Transgressions that could excommunicate him or send him to prison. For spite, I add visions of the fiery pit he fears more than death. His brain freezes in recognition.

We've met before.

"Miss De Lucio and I need to be on our way. As she said, we do not require your company." The sound of my voice makes him visibly shudder. For many years, I've had a starring role in his worst nightmares. When I shake his hand, I let him gaze upon his future death. It's not pretty.

Livia's mouth falls open. She's too nice for her own good.

"You'll be on your way now, won't you?" I nod and force him to nod with me.

"Yes!" His voice returns and he grasps his throat. "I just remembered I have an appointment in an hour." Bowing in deference as he retreats, he stumbles over a potted plant and nearly falls to the floor.

Livia frowns, turns to me, then back to the bishop. "Thank you for understanding. Please join us for dinner."

I discreetly shake my head and send him running to his car. "Thank you, Miss De Lucio. But I'll be busy all day."

Livia lifts her eyes to mine. "What did you do? Did you threaten him behind my back? He looked scared out of his mind."

"Do I look threatening?" I smile as my gaze falls on her pouty lips. She's so lovely.

"I've got my eye on you, Mr. Angeli. No funny business at the abbey." She winks. "And thank you for helping me out. Some clergy can be misogynistic. They'll take orders from a man, but not a woman."

"You're welcome. I'm at your disposal." I lead her down the path and open the car door. "Shall we?"

15

LIVIA

HE'S A MONSTER. NO ONE IS PERFECT, BUT THIS IS BEYOND THE pale. A member of the clergy must be above reproach and Bishop Ambrose Moore was a disgrace to himself, to the church and above all, to God. Last night, Luca confirmed a premonition that's disturbed me since the start of his candidacy. His soul has not passed to heaven. Now that we've spoken to the sisters, I am one hundred percent certain we cannot proceed with his beatification, much less sainthood. I've never investigated anyone less worthy.

As we walk towards the car, Sister Odette grips my trembling hand and wipes the flood of tears streaming down her cheeks. I'm grateful she didn't hear it all. She couldn't hear the torment in their minds or feel the terror of their memories. When I couldn't bear another minute, Luca took over.

I underestimated his compassion and kindness. My heart swelled with each caring gesture and every thoughtful word he spoke to comfort them in their time of need. I won't forget his kindness.

Before we reach the car, she stops short to give me news. "I spoke to Cardinal Bertolucci when I stepped out of the room. I could hardly utter the words to describe what we heard or the torment these women endured. But he needs to know everything before he arrives in York." Her voice shakes with grief as she fights to finish her sentence. "He's appalled. Cardinal Lunetta is furious. They plan to speak to His Holiness before they leave Rome."

I nod and lift my hand to massage my chest, trying in vain to slow the beat of my thundering heart. I don't know what I'll do if they proceed with his candidacy. I know the Cardinals will fight to quash it, but Moore has many champions. Not all members of the Holy See put church politics aside.

If they ignore my recommendations, I'll resign. I can't in good faith help elevate a man who abused his position, violated innocent women and broke the sanctity of his office. This is a good job, but there are more important things in life than money or prestige. I won't take part in anyone's charade.

"I just spoke to Bertolucci. There's been a change of plans." Luca catches up and helps us into the car. Sister Odette remains distraught, but the sight of him warms my punctured heart and soothes my spirit. I couldn't have made it through today without him. He endured the brunt of their heartbreaking confessions and kept his composure where I failed.

"Change of plans?" We glide into the backseat and he takes the seat next to the driver.

He nods. "Sister, please call the Cardinal as soon as you can. He wants you to meet him in York when he arrives tomorrow afternoon. He wants Livia and I to follow a new lead outside Paris. The sisters here provided me with names to add to our list of interviewees." He hands me the note and I glare sullenly at the names of six new nuns.

"Are you up for more?" Luca's voice cuts through my listless haze and draws my weary eyes to his. I'm not up for it. Nuns give their lives, youth and dreams of motherhood to serve the church. I could never sacrifice so much.

They could not conceal their misplaced shame. The despair in their voices will haunt me for years. I can't let them down. We need to chase every lead and compile every ounce of ammunition against Moore's candidacy.

"I'll be fine. I'll take some time to recuperate tonight. This is too important to neglect." I release a heavy sigh and sink into my seat. When my eyes find his, a soft smile appears on his beautiful face and my heart melts. Where did this man come from? How could someone so perfect exist? Perfect for me.

Does he think I'm perfect for him?

I do. His voice appears in my mind.

Oh my God, he heard me.

Amid my harrowing dismay, I forgot to seal the vault. I'm mortified. *Absolutely mortified.* How could I be so careless? Shutting him out, I avoid his gaze and stare out the car window. He must have heard every word of praise. Images of him, unnecessarily shirtless, while he cradled our babies to sleep in those massive arms were laid bare. I can't face him. I'll never be able to face him again.

In a moment of madness, I graze my fingers on the door handle and contemplate jumping out of a moving car. It's a fleeting thought. Nothing will change. He won't forget my words and with my luck, I'll land face first.

"Livia?" His divine tenor grabs my attention.

"Yes?" I clear my throat, fearful of every word that might tumble out. I need to play it cool. He doesn't know what he saw. I could have been replaying a movie in my mind. *Yeah, a movie.* I like movies. There must be tons of movies with half-naked men rocking newborn babies to sleep.

I'm blowing this way out of proportion.

"Don't forget I have a surprise for you. After you've had time to rest and recharge your batteries, change into comfortable clothes. I want to show you something. I promise, you'll love it." He winks.

My jaw drops. Oh, no. *A surprise?* I can't be alone with him. He knows my indifference is just an act. He knows I fantasize about him. He knows I dream of having a horde of Luca Angeli babies with his dark eyes and beautiful full lips. One kiss and he'll talk me into a sinful night of passionate love that hurls me into moral collapse. I can't go. *I won't.*

This ends here and now.

"Livia?" His eyes twinkle with a hint of naughtiness and my trembling thighs clench.

"Will I need a coat?" I'm pathetic.

16

LUCIFER

"Are you ready?" I lean my shoulder against her door frame and gaze adoringly into her trusting blue eyes. My lovesick heart wants to confess but every minute we spend together sends my mind reeling with the inevitability of her rejection.

I can't bear it. *Not yet.*

When her soft smile appears, I fight the urge to take her in my arms and throw her sweet, wholesome body on the bed. It's tortuous, but for once I won't think of my needs first.

She nods. "I am. Thanks for giving me extra time. I was desperate for a hot bath." She locks her door and gives me her hand, winding her fingers through mine.

"I hoped it helped you unwind." My heart flutters as visions of Livia's naked body invade my thoughts. Within seconds, my cock comes to life.

"It did. Should we check on Sister Odette before we depart?" She curls a loose strand of hair around her ear and wraps her scarf around her neck. Now that she's out of her suit, she takes on a childish air that enhances her innocence. I don't think she's ever looked so beautiful.

"She left to meet a friend. They're having an early dinner in town. She didn't give a name. She just said it's someone she hasn't seen in years." I lead her downstairs and stop near the door to retrieve our coats.

While we walk, our eyes remained fixed on one another, lost in a trance of lust and the promise of so much more. I need to make this right before we take it farther. She should know the truth. She needs to know I can change. I am changing.

For her, I'll do anything.

But what will the truth cost me?

"Let me help you with that." I take her winter coat off the hook and hold it open. She giggles to herself and sneaks in one arm after the next. Before she has a chance to fasten it, I spin her around, button each button and pull her hat over her head. She's adorable. Every time I look at her sweet face, my heart threatens to explode.

Earlier, she let me into her mind. I shouldn't have pried, but I don't claim to be perfect. I'm a fallen angel in love for the first time with a woman far out of his reach. I believe she loves Luca Angeli. She sees a future with him. She's envisioned a wedding, babies, and a quaint house in the Italian countryside. All the things I want to give her, but she sees them with him.

Will she love me, too? How can I tell? I understand pride and vanity. It comes naturally for me. Love does not. Lust and marital love are mortal emotions. You were created with a drive to procreate. I was not.

Until Livia, I never gave it a second thought.

I can't believe I've succumbed so quickly. I'm not ashamed. Just bewildered. Three days ago, I wanted nothing to do with humans and now...now what? Do I want to become one? Could I? Others have surrendered their immortality for less. I'd do it for her... if she'll have me. If she can see beyond my past and trust me to love her.

I can do this. *I can be good.* With her, I know I can live a virtuous life. I'm not a prisoner of my circumstances. I want to be who she sees. Livia's angelic bloodline lets her sense darkness. But she doesn't sense it in me.

Maybe I'm not so far gone.

Whenever I'm near her, I feel the light I once carried break through my heavy cloak of rage. My heart feels lighter than air. My spirit feels renewed. Because of her, I feel reborn. The only power I crave is the strength to keep her safe and the courage to love her the way she deserves to be loved.

We can live the quiet life she wants, devoid of sin. After all, once we're married, all these delicious urges festering in my mind are legitimately sanctioned. One could say I'm duty-bound to fulfill them. She wants a family. Pleasure and procreation go hand in hand.

That sounds right.

She slides into the front seat and I close the door behind her. The last time we were completely alone, I couldn't control myself. I'll be better today. I'm not an animal incapable of harnessing his darker impulses. I'll woo her properly. There's no rush.

"Where are we going?" Her blue eyes sparkle with a trace of newfound admiration, and I can't hold back. With absolutely no finesse, I lunge across the console, seize her lips and sate my ravenous hunger. Her soft lips and delicate moan fuel my boundless desire to make her mine. My brain buzzes with longing. When I pull away, her dreamy eyes lock to mine and I snatch her back in, too aroused to be gentle. Possessing her lips, my tongue intertwines with hers and sexual adrenaline flows through me.

Kissing my way down the line of her neck, I graze her supple skin with my teeth and tug her harder into my embrace. Her breasts crash against my chest and her eyes widen with surprise. Before she can stop me, I skim my trembling hands down her back and caress the curve of the most phenomenal behind I've ever seen.

"What am I going to do with you, Livia?" I whisper against her cheek as I fight to regain my composure.

Her breath hitches. "What do you want to do?"

"Fucking everything."

17

LIVIA

As soon as I step out of the car, the sound of crashing waves and the icy breeze of the North Atlantic assault my senses. Seagulls caw overhead and the salt in the air sticks to my wool coat. I thought we were hiking the Cliffs of Moher, but we passed the visitors center ten minutes ago. "Where are you taking me?"

He offers his hand. "Bundle up. We're going for a walk." His smile broadens. "Trust me. You need this."

I nod and follow him. There's no reason I should put so much faith in a man I hardly know. I can't read his thoughts. He could toss me over the precipice ahead and I'd never see it coming. Con artists are everywhere. I know better. But there's something about him that keeps me glued to his side. He's familiar. *Did I know him in a past life?* From the moment he first shook my hand, I felt a strange but deep recognition. Like meeting him was unavoidable or predestined. I don't understand it, and for once, I may not care.

With my hand grasping his, he leads us into a downward path of rocky steps. I walk with trepidation, fearful I'll slip on the ocean mist that's gathered on the stones, but my feet stay firmly grounded. Every step seems to dry before I touch it, and the steeper we go, the more the ground beneath appears to level off.

It's the strangest thing, but I'm too anxious to question it. Nothing takes me off my course. By the time we're halfway down, we've broken into a light sprint, laughing as the mist from broken waves splash into our faces.

When we reach the bottom, we exit through a small tunnel that meets the narrow shore. We can't go far. Less than ten feet away, the violent waves of the frigid Atlantic water engulf water-smoothed rocks and with every passing minute the tide threatens to take us in.

Speechless and mesmerized, I squeeze Luca's hand tighter and crane my neck to gaze into his cheerful face. "Why did you bring me here?" I'm grateful but confused. This hardly seems safe, and it's not exactly what I expected from a second date.

"Don't you like it?" His smile fades, but the twinkle in his eyes remain.

My heart flies off the cliff in a reckless free fall and lands forever changed. I know I've fallen in love. How could I help myself? He's unspeakably beautiful. He's kind, sexy and smart. No other man could ever compare to the perfection before me. All that remains is for my heart to convince my brain to let go.

"Of course, I do. But why here? This feels dangerous. Beautiful but dangerous." I lean into his body for warmth and he unbuttons his coat to let me wind my arms around his waist.

With a breathy sigh, he holds me tightly and shields me from the savage wind. "You can't stay in your safe space forever. Besides, the most dangerous things are often the most beautiful."

"Like what?" I don't understand.

"Like love." He bends down and kisses my forehead. "I love you, Livia. No matter the consequences. I love you."

"Love?"

18

LUCIFER

Running through the rain, I hold my coat over our heads and whisk her through the front door of the inn. A blast of warm air strikes our faces and melts the ice settling into our bones. Livia's messy hair clings to her brow as she looks up with a playful smile. Even in her disheveled state, she takes my breath away.

"You're soaked. Let me take care of you." The lump in my throat makes me stammer as I lead her into the sitting room and place her directly in front of the raging fire. She fusses but complies without too much lip.

"You're being silly. I'm not that wet." Her teeth chatter as she speaks. She's such a liar. White lies still count, but they're not enough. Deep down, I'd wish she'd do more. I can feel the noose tightening.

Lucifer's happy. That can't stand for much longer. *Someone needs to fly in to destroy it.*

"Indulge me. It's my fault we were out." I peel off her damp coat and tug her close. When she winds her arms around my waist and cradles her head against my chest, my heart soars. I don't need for her to say it. I can feel it. I could feel her heart race every time we kissed. Her warmth and affection radiate from her spirit into mine.

"Why are you so warm? You're as toasty as a marshmallow." She digs her face into my sweater and her taut nipples graze against the thin fabric. My mouth waters with wolfish lust. When her eyes find mine, her pupils widen, drowning me in those pale blue pools. I can wait for her to say it, but I don't think I can wait to make love to her.

"Marshmallow? Explain yourself." I kiss the top of her head and breathe her in. Intoxicated by her innocence, my mind spins like a top. I've never wanted anyone or anything as much as I want this. I'm desperate for Livia.

This is the only redemption I crave. Love redeems. I never believed it. But until now, I never understood its power. When her mouth parts to speak, I lift her face and take every centimeter of her plump pink lips as my own. She gasps with surprise, mortified by such a public display of affection, then swiftly melts into my arms.

In the depths of a blistering kiss, our breaths mingle, and my hands roam every curve of her glorious body. The ache grows deeper. With each kiss, Livia fills the emptiness and calms my spirit. When a faint moan escapes her lips, my heart grows in proportion to the stiff cock obscenely tenting my jeans.

"Livia?" The sound of Sister Odette's voice makes Livia fly backwards and nearly knock over a lamp.

"Oh, my God." The flush on her face deepens.

"Forgive me for interrupting. I just wanted to speak to you before I retire for the evening. I have an early flight." No judgmental glances or snide remarks. My hands were resting on Livia's ass when she barged in. For a nun, she's surprisingly open-minded.

"Yes?" Humiliated by her behavior, Livia squeaks her reply.

It was a kiss. We're adults. This little girl needs to loosen up. She needs dick. Mine. *Only mine.*

"I just spoke with Cardinal Lunetta who received a message from Inspector La Rosa before he flew out. He wants you to know they found Lionel Clemson's body. Poor soul must have met his match. It was most horrific. I don't want to give you nightmares, my dear. But I want to set your mind at ease." She shakes her head with remorse and makes the sign of the cross.

Livia's brow furrows and her gaze drifts off into the distance. "Lionel Clemson? Who's Lionel Clemson?"

Sister Odette raises her palms in surprise. "Oh, my goodness, Livia! You truly are working yourself to death. Clemson is the young man who sat next to you on your flight. The one you believed wanted to harm you. How on earth did you forget?"

Fuck.

Livia's shoulders slump. "Lionel... Clemson?" She scratches her head. "Plane?"

The sister moves closer, her expression riddled with concern. I don't blame her, but it's not Livia's fault. I erased all memory of Lionel. I didn't realize she'd told others about him. "Luca, did she eat?"

I freeze, fearful the sound of my voice will trigger her memories. Nodding, I mumble my words. "We just had dinner."

"Get some rest, dear. You're pushing yourself too hard. You don't have to save the world on your own. Luca will help you." She pats Livia's cheek and winks at me.

While we watch her walk away, Livia's eyes glaze over with anxiety. "Luca? Why don't I remember? That's not like me. I can hardly remember flying to Rome, but I know I got on the plane." She scrambles for her purse and yanks out a wrinkled boarding pass. "See?"

I run my fingers through her hair and caress her face. "I'm sure you're just overwhelmed. It was a traumatic day. Go upstairs and get ready for bed."

Her eyes grow wide. "You're not coming? I mean... to your room. Not to mine." She fidgets. "You know what I mean."

I nod and plant a soft kiss on her lips. "I'll come up to say goodnight in a few minutes. There's something I need to take care of first." She smiles and scurries away, embarrassed that she almost propositioned me.

I'm such a prick. I could have eased her worries, but I can't confess like this. Not here. Not with an audience of angels looking on.

"That was sweet." Azazel smirks and warms his hands by the fire.

"Outside." I growl and point at the front door.

"Outside? It's raining outside." Samael whines, dragging his feet across the carpet.

"Now." Malphas rests his hands on their shoulders and pushes them forward.

"This better not be a fucking social call."

*　*　*

AZAZEL STANDS on the roof's precarious incline as he lights a cigarette and takes a long drag. His mouth parts then shuts. Then parts again. "Samael has news."

"Samael? Why are all three of you here? Did you come to gawk? Does my relationship amuse you?" My brow furrows with exasperation. This must be the juiciest piece of gossip buzzing through heaven and earth.

Lucifer's in love.

They slowly shake their head in unison. Anxiety painted garishly on their faces.

"Samael didn't want to come alone." Malphas uncrosses his arms. "It's not good, Lucifer. He knows you. We know what happens when you receive unpleasant news." He pushes Samael and makes him stumble a few feet in front of me. "Get on with it."

I nod and grind my teeth with anger. If they know, why are they making me wait? "Well? Why do you always make things difficult on yourself? Spit it out."

"I spoke to Calla." He cringes as he speaks, as if each word pains him to utter. "It's not good."

"Calla?"

"The guardian." Azazel chimes in, nervously swaying in the wind.

"Get on with it. I'm growing more furious by the second." I clench my fist and slam it into the opposite hand. My patience thins. There is no doubt they're here to deliver horrible news, but nothing good can come from dragging it out. Whatever punishment comes from angering me will come either way.

Azazel and Malphas back away, leaving Samael in the foreground. He looks over his shoulder and shrinks, shivering with fear. My pulse spikes. *How bad can it be?* I'm already expecting the worst.

"For God's sake!" A growl from the pit of my stomach shrieks past my clenched teeth and blows all three off the roof. Blue fire scorches the tips of their wings as debris strikes their faces. They scramble mid air and grip each other for purchase. With a quick spring, they jump back to their feet, put out their singed feather and brush themselves off.

Enraged and eager to leave, Malphas swats an errant ember and growls. "It's not just a question of keeping her, Lucifer. Samael has been tasked with bringing her in. She's on borrowed time. She doesn't belong here anymore."

Before the last word drips off his tongue, my knees give out and I crash into the stone shingles below me. The air leaves my lungs. My heart stops beating. One by one, Malphas, Samael and Azazel drop like flies, deprived of breath, clutching their hearts and held in place by the depths of my grief. They reach out, begging for release and whimpering in submission, but I can't see them. I'm blinded by rage. Consumed by the deepish anguish I've ever known.

How can I spend eternity without her?

I fall forward on my hands, incapacitated by a visceral pain that tears through my heart and rips my soul in two. I won't surrender her to death. All this time I've lived incomplete. My empty spirit existed without joy. Bitterness was constant. Rage was my only comfort. Now that I finally found someone that makes this brutal world bearable, they want me to give her up. *I can't.* That's the cruelest thing they've ever asked me to do.

"Leave me." My voice booms and the vibration releases them from my grip. All three fall, writhing in agony and shocked by my refusal.

We don't go against heaven. We play by the rules we're given.

But not me. Not anymore.

Gasping for air, Samael tries to speak. "I have no choice, Lucifer. She's overdue. If I don't do it, someone else will."

"If you touch her, I'll kill you. You know I can. You are not beyond my reach. And when I'm finished with you, I'll annihilate your little girlfriend. Do we understand one another?" When he feels my hand squeeze his windpipe, he nods.

"They don't have to do this. Nothing is set in stone. If it were, I wouldn't have been able to save her." With a wave of my hand I blow them off the roof and into the clouds.

If heaven wants her, they'll have to come through me.

19

LIVIA

I'm not naïve to love. I've had boyfriends. I've dated. Things didn't get physical because I didn't reciprocate their feelings, but whatever they felt was never as intense as the emotions simmering off Luca Angeli.

This is wild but familiar. Oddly familiar. And ridiculously sublime.

We met three days ago, but I feel like I've seen his face before. His dark gray eyes bear an intimacy I can't explain. I could be imagining it. He's gorgeous. He's a hot Italian man and I have a predilection for hot Italian men. Perhaps I'm injecting an otherworldly significance to my raging hormones to make me feel better.

I've got nerve. I'm downright shameless. Hugging, rubbing, kissing, trailing my fingers on his rippled abdomen while I held him for warmth. And how can I forget Sister Odette catching me with Luca's big mitts on my ass? No, shameless doesn't even begin to describe my behavior today. But is it love? If it's love, maybe it's not so shameless.

Does he love me? He says he does. Men don't say it willy-nilly. His kiss felt sincere. His eyes didn't appear false.

But what the hell do I know? My experience is limited. And not entirely by choice.

Sometimes I think the only reason I've been so good for so long is because I've lived with a constant audience. I mean, it's hard to give in to passion when you see angels lurking in every corner? I swear I try to be good for the sake of being good. But I'm a woman. I have needs. I'm just not comfortable making love in front of spectators.

Of course, no one's around anymore.

It feels odd. I've been so thrilled with the privacy, I haven't questioned it. And yet, I can't help but wonder if it has something to do with Luca. He sees them too. Does he have powers I don't? Can he make them disappear? This could be a godsend. My father longed for this. If Luca has the power to make them go away, he's worth holding on to forever.

I glance at my watch, peek out the door and decide I may have time for a bath. It's nothing illicit. I'm not prepping for sex. It rained on me. I'm chilled to the bone and need to bring up my temperature.

Why am I talking to myself? No one's watching me anymore. If I want a bath, I'll take a damn bath.

Strutting into the bathroom with an air of defiance, I strip off my sweater and switch on the faucet. Anxious to sink in, I run my hand back and forth through the water and pull down my leggings. When a rush of cold air prickles my skin, I sprint back into the room to light the tiny fireplace. I'm out of my element in Ireland. New York won't get this dreary for another month and I'm a wimp in cold weather.

I strike a match. The blue flame flickers, then instantly extinguishes. I glance at the window to check if a breeze has seeped through, but its sealed shut. Shaking my head, I strike it again. This time the flame lingers and I gaze mesmerized as it rises into a thin vertical line. My eyes grow wide and I hop back as it dances, drifting slowly like a fiery snake as it winds its way around my head.

Hypnotized by the light, I'm too dazed to be afraid. It floats seductively against my skin, charming me with sparkles of light until my lips part and I inhale the scent. I smile to myself. It tastes like Luca. It an odd way, it feels like Luca.

The flickering flame falls into my palm and the blue fire grows, washing over me like soft kisses. It whirls into the form of a hand as it surrounds and winds its way around my arms, legs, through my thighs and over my breasts. As it warms my flesh, it dampens my core and my dewy skin tingles with sexual desire.

I should be afraid, but I'm not.

Something in the wavering light soothes me into an eerie calm that sinks deep into my soul. The only image my mind will conjure is him. His hands. His lips take the place of the fire that now consumes every inch of my body.

I could live in this fire forever.

The sound of water breaks the spell. Confused, I run back into the bathroom, just before the water reaches the edge of the tub. Baffled by the lost time, I release a few inches of water and try to remember how I got so sweaty. My eyes dart to the fire smoldering across the room and ponder if I stood too close when I lit it.

Did I light it? *When did I light it?*

I slap my cheek. *Livia! You're losing it.*

Massaging my forehead, I take a take deep breath and struggle to calm my heavy heart. It's been a rough day. I shouldn't be too hard on myself.

With a withered sigh, I step into the tub and sink into the steamy water. It's divine. I need this. I need to clear my head and think sensibly about my life. And about Luca.

He's wonderful. Any woman would find him irresistible. But I need to think like a sensible person again. Whenever I'm in his presence, my mind turns to mush. My ovaries overrule my brain and my heart beats only for him. If things get one teensy bit hotter, I'll submit to passion and cross into an unknown realm.

I don't know this realm, but Luca makes me want to leap into it. He makes me want to lose myself into a world I've never known. If he leads, I'll follow him anywhere.

What am I saying? No, I won't. *Yes, you will.*

No, I won't.

Yes, you know you will.

As blistering thoughts of Luca weaken me, I lean back and let the hot water skim my shoulders. Warmth surrounds every part of me, soothing away the long day and lulling me into drowsiness. Closing my eyes, my mind skips the harshness of the abbey and I lazily drift into daydreams of ocean spray and words of love.

Vivid memories of Luca's soft lips and dark eyes overrun my thoughts. I graze my fingers across my mouth and whisper his name, aroused to hear it out loud. Desperate for his touch, I trail my finger across my shoulders, down the length of my biceps and skim my forearms, imagining his sinewy hands in their place.

The room grows hotter.

Lost in a haze of lust, I rub my cheek against my shoulder and smooth both hands across my chest. My palms repeatedly graze my tight nipples, but they're too small to cover my breasts. I think of Luca's hands. I bet I'd lose sight of my breasts in his giant hands.

What would he do? How would he feel?

Sinking deeper into the water, my lids droop and my thoughts wander further. Steel-gray eyes appear in my mind. Watery hands envelop my flesh as trickles of water stream down my face.

When I open my eyes, blue flames have enveloped the room and a pair of arms pull me out just in time.

Luca.

20

LUCIFER

Too frantic to care, I transport through her locked door. I don't care if she screams. I'll explain myself. But I need to see her. She needs to be near me. Every moment we're apart gives them time to steal her away. And I won't let that happen.

Livia's mine. *All mine.*

Stepping through, I hear a hum coming from a second room. Fearful of frightening her, I stay by the door. I wish I could take my time. Livia deserves better. She deserves music and dancing. She should have flowers and poorly written love letters she can throw in my face when I make her angry.

But there's no time for that. And there's no time for a long-drawn-out confession. If I want Livia, I need to make her mine, here and now.

I know she loves me. I hope she can accept who I am. If she rejects me, if she runs, she'll meet whatever death they've planned for her.

I can't bear that. I've forfeited my redemption. I can't forfeit her too.

When she saunters in from the bathroom naked as the day she

was born, my brain freezes. My heart sputters to a halt. She's a vision. Every inch of her is indescribably beautiful. Every valley swerves into ripe mountains. Every delicious curve swoops into mouthwatering plains. Her round ample behind jiggles with every step, in concert with the sweet bounce of her voluptuous breasts.

I swallow hard and rub the front of my pants, easing the iron rod digging into my zipper. With her back to me, I shed my sweater. Between the sweltering room and Livia's sweet body, I can hardly catch my breath. Fortunately, she's too preoccupied to see my jaw wide open. She can't see the saliva dripping down my chin. And God forbid she catches me peel off the rest of my clothes.

Too dizzy to speak, I vanish into the bookcase and take its form. If she tries hard enough, she could see me. But she's let her guard down. She's not expecting to see anything. As fiendish as I feel, this is my chance to take the upper hand. And I need all the help I can get if I want to save her.

Dumbstruck by the sight of her gorgeous body and speechless with love, I watch her strike a match. From my place across the room, I blow it out.

I'm not sure why. I'm still working on my plan.

She looks around, curious if a draft has drifted in from a gap in the window. In that moment, I move closer and hover overhead. When she strikes a second match, I emerge as its flame. It's the closest thing to her. Something that can touch her.

I flicker into a blue orb. She tilts her head and smiles when she thinks she sees my eyes in the fire. Curious, she stares deeper and the darkness reflected in the flame hypnotizes her into a waking dream. When she blinks, the flame moves above her. She doesn't see my chest rise above hers. When the fire flickers into her face and touches her lips, she doesn't see my mouth cover hers, but I know she tastes me. I read her thoughts and see my face in her mind.

All she sees is the flame. She can't see my hungry hands roam every inch of her supple breasts. She feels the fire tickle the sensitive flesh of her rosy tipped nipples, but she can't see my mouth suckling greedily while my hand explores the slick apex of her thighs. She doesn't know it's me turning her soft skin to gooseflesh.

She whispers my name in her mind. No, not my name. *His name.* The name I gave her.

A pang of jealousy strikes. *It's ludicrous.* That's the only name she knows. I want to hear her say Lucifer. Luca isn't real. Lucifer loves her. Only Lucifer.

My fit distracts her. She remembers the water, breaks free from my spell and darts away. With my heart thumping furiously and my cock harder than steel, I follow.

Trudging slowly into the bathroom, I search my mind for an alternative plan. This is only a hiccup. I can think on my feet and make her fall in love with the real me.

But how?

I look up and feast my weary eyes on the woman I love, and everything comes together. It's not perfect, but Livia's beauty inspires me. Like it did from the start.

Angels have always been voyeurs.

Some of us are messengers. Most of us are watchers or guardians. For some angels, watching is their favorite part. Malphas and Asmodeus rave about it. They can't get enough. They love watching human females. All types. All sizes. Women fascinate them. I never understood or shared their inclinations. But then again, I never saw Livia.

She's magnificent. Even more beautiful in the light. No artist could ever capture her beauty. And none ever will.

I take in the sight of her pale skin enveloped by the hot water and marvel as it turns a sharp shade of pink. Steam floats off the water. As she sinks lower, her buoyant breasts rise and I glimpse the flesh bobbing just above the surface, calling for my attention...my hands...my mouth.

With my face in her mind and my name on her tongue, she runs her hands along her body, caressing each curve. She simmers with sexual longing but can't sate desires she doesn't understand. Salivating to indulge in her flesh, I lose my earthly confines and I sink into the water. My spirit joins the water and blue fire spreads along the surface. I spread her legs around mine and my hand forms around hers. She thinks she's dreaming. Whimpering with need and longing for things she's too frightened to say, she tosses her head back and whispers my name.

She loves me. I can feel it in her mind. I can hear it in every beat of her heart. But the truth is coming back. That first day is coming back and I panic.

Flames rise from the water. Smoke descends from the ceiling, covering us both as I lift her into my arms and carry her out. She's confused. Her listless gaze searches mine for answers, but she loses herself in the trance of the blue flames.

As soon as we cross the threshold to her bedroom, the flames extinguish, and her body stiffens as she stirs out of a dream. She could push me away. My behavior's shocking and inappropriate. I've jumped hurdles past the lines of propriety. We're both naked and wet. She won't remember how we reached this point. For all she knows, I've drugged her and for some reason bathed her before taking advantage of her.

"Luca...what..." Her breathless words cut off as my mouth covers hers. Her taste summons a thousand words I'm too choked up to speak. Hopeful that she might accept me, I carry her into the bed and slide us in.

"Livia, I love you. They want to take you away from me. I can't lose you." Tears flood as words tumble out without thought. I don't know what's gotten into me, but true love makes me incapable of duplicity. She needs to know everything. She needs to know who loves her.

Her dazed expression deepens and a wicked smile curves across her face. Her pale eyes darken with lust. When her wet body presses to mine, my darkness swirls around her and mingles with her light. Shadows consume her, dropping her inhibitions and fears.

"Do you remember me?" I whisper as I bring my mouth to hers. Our tongues dance, licking and delving deep as we mine for each other's souls. She's not under a spell. *Livia's unleashed.* She's lived her entire life in the light, she's an inherently good soul, but I recently discovered she's a descendant of Asmodeus, my second lieutenant and the demon of lust. Whatever he is, lives somewhere deep in her.

She shakes her head, then nods. "Black wings? I remember. Who are you?"

I growl and swing her into my lap. "Don't you know?" Squeezing her breasts together, I encase my face in her cleavage and inhale her scent like the filthiest dope fiend hungry for his fix. I could lose my mind with Livia.

Suckling and tugging each nipple while she whimpers in my arms, I listen to the beat of her racing heart and ask again. "Tell me you know who I am."

She lifts my chin and examines my face. "Luca Angeli? I should have known. The *Angel of Light?* Luca, if you are who you are, how can I love you? Lucifer doesn't love. Lucifer is Hate. Pride and Rage." Her expression saddens.

She knows who I am. She knows who I am, and she loves me. *She doesn't want to love me.* But she does.

"Lucifer never knew how to love. But he loves you. And I know you love me, Livia. And you'll never get away from me." I growl, wind my fingers through her dark hair, and crush her shocked lips to mine. When our tongues meet, her whimpers transforms to moans.

She attempts a weak protest, but I've had enough. She's mine. Her heart knows it. Her body wants it. But her judicious mind needs to accept it. Not one to shrink from a challenge, I toss her back on the mattress, spread her knees and sink my mouth into her wetness.

The first taste seizes my senses and overwhelms a primal instinct I shouldn't have. Livia's ripe. This union could bear fruit. For the first time I feel the urge every mortal man feels when he claims a woman he loves. The drive to breed. I want that with Livia. I want to spill my seed inside her fertile body and watch it grow. I want to build generations with her.

"Tell me you want me, Livia. Say it." I swipe my tongue against her clit and she tenses her thighs on my shoulders. A faint cry of pleasure flies from her lips as my tongue conquers her body, stabbing as I feast. She wants to scream, but she's too afraid to give in to me. She fears losing herself in the depths of passion means losing her soul.

The flush on her skin travels from her breasts to her face as she bites her cherry pink lips and hums. She tries to muffle her cries, but with every flick of my tongue, her arousal grows. A vixen lies in wait under her angelic veneer and the more our spirits entwine, the more her hunger matures.

When I use my teeth to graze her sensitive skin, suctioning on her clit without mercy, she slaps her hand over her mouth and falls into the abyss of an earth-shattering orgasm. Winding her fingers through my hair, she tries in vain to hold me still.

"You're mine, Livia. You've always been mine. I won't lose you." I gaze at the woman I love, lost in a trance of desire and wanton abandonment. This is new for her. Her eyes search the room. Her hands reach for mine, unsure of what to do or what to feel. All she knows is she wants more.

"Luca..." She whispers.

"Don't call me that... it's not my name." I rise to my knees and run my cock through her soaked slit. Her eyes grow twice their size, but she spreads her thighs and pulls me closer.

"Tell me you love me." I smooth my hands across her breasts and take her hand in mine. When her blue eyes find mine, my heart breaks and mends in a different shape and beat. It's Livia's heart. I'm completely hers. I'm completely in love. I can't live another day without her.

"I won't let anyone hurt you. Ever." The look in her eyes takes my breath away.

"Why me?" She runs her delicate fingers down my back and sighs. Her eyes mist, but I'm not sure if it's sadness or joy.

"You redeem me. Love redeems me." I kiss her gently and ask her the question I asked her our first night together. "Can you fall in love with me, Livia?"

A small cry escapes her beautiful lips. "I already have... but how..."

"Don't think about it...for now...trust me." I slide into her, one inch at a time, trembling as our souls collide and her warm, tight channel squeezes my cock with the grip of her innocence. My muscles tighten, and my body vibrates, humming with divine pleasure as I stretch her open, savoring every second of Livia's corruption. This is different than the others. This is for me and me alone. Livia's heart is pure. But her days of living like a saint are over.

With a high-pitched moan that makes my hair stand on end, my girl welcomes me into her body. Pleasure overruns my senses. Love steals my breath. With every frantic pump, her celestial light absorbs the darkness embedded in me and my heart soars higher with an unconditional love I haven't felt since the dawn of time.

"Tell me you love me. I can't lose you, Livia." Too overcome to wait for her reply, our mouths crash as my cock sinks deeper inside her, driving hard as I claim every inch.

She pulls away and nods. "I love you. You're not wicked. I know you're not wicked. Please don't be bad anymore." She whimpers, the innocence in her voice warms my heart.

I shake my head and hold her face in my hands. "I'm an angel. I've fallen halfway. I'll fall all the way for you. If they let me. I'll be Luca Angeli. I'll live and die as your husband. I've never wanted anything more."

She hiccups a soft cry, then seals her lips to mine. "Lucifer..."

The sound of my name makes my heart soar. "Livia, marry me. I'll find a way to get it done in the morning." I don't know what will happen after tomorrow. I don't know if they'll steal her away in her sleep. But I want to know for one precious day I had a wife and if we're married on consecrated ground, Livia will always be tied to me. Even if we're apart, I'll always be able to feel her.

When she gasps a faint *yes*, I bury myself deep. She grips my shoulders, screaming with a mix of pain and pleasure as I mold her body to mine. Steadying myself inside her, I relish the way she grips my cock. With every thrust, my arousal grows stronger, for her and for us.

I can't give her up. I can't let her go. She's claimed me as hers forever.

"I don't have much time. Do I?" Fear pools in her big blue eyes.

My heart sinks. She knows. She always knows too much. Her sight will be the death of me. I brush my lips against hers and take them in a slow, passionate kiss. She's my heart. I won't let her be afraid.

"As long as we're on earth, Lucifer reigns supreme. And as long as you're with me, they can't touch you. No one will hurt you." I wrap her arms around my neck and watch her eyes grow impossibly wide. Black wings unfurl and stretch out across the small room.

Grinding fiercely, I wind her legs around my hips and lift us into the air, hovering just over the bed. To make love as an angel is beyond taboo. But I don't care. Livia is my love, and this is who I am.

Flying, fucking, and kissing, I hold us, curling my wings to keep her body tucked to mine. My muscles clench and spasm with each plunge, but the discomfort is worth it. The more I thrust, the wilder she becomes.

"Lucifer..." With her thighs locked tightly around my hips, Livia pumps wildly, thrashing mercilessly on my cock while her supple breasts bounce salaciously in my face.

She's a goddess.

Twirling her around, I thrust with hunger, frantically plunging until we shatter in a seismic fit of ecstasy that sends us flying across the room.

"Oh my God..." She withers into my chest.

"Please, don't mention him."

21
LIVIA

This feels like a dream. A nightmare? No, not a nightmare. This is what I want. These past few days have been the happiest ones of my life, and he's the reason. Luca. No, Lucifer.

Say it, Livia. You fell in love with Lucifer.

What kind of wicked girl falls in love with the devil? What kind of tramp surrenders her flower to Satan? It's worse! I've agreed to marry the Prince of Darkness.

He's *my* prince. The love of my life. All those years I saw his face in my dreams. All that time I waited for darkness to steal me away in the night. And I was waiting for him. He's the other half of my soul. I never realized how empty I felt until he came along and filled me.

Oh, my goodness, not like that. *Heavens.* Well, not entirely like that.

"Are you ready my love?" Luca takes my hand and his sweet smile pulls my heartstrings. My dry mouth waters.

I nod and let my trembling fingers skitter into his palm. "Are you sure? It's much too soon. The church requires six months. I've read about this before."

His eyes flash red. "I have the power of persuasion, Livia. Don't make me use it on you, too." He wags his eyebrows and chuckles.

I cover my heart, surprised by the sudden dampening between my thighs. How have I fallen so fast? "Luca?"

His eyes narrow.

"Sorry. Lucifer. Where will we live? I don't want to live..." I point to the floor. I've heard rumors of a spiritual plane here on earth, a purgatory where souls wait to be reborn, but since he's the first angel who's ever spoken to me, there was no way to confirm.

He licks his lips and smiles. "There is no..." He points to the floor. "Hell is all around us. I live in New York. But we can live in Italy... in the country." He winks.

I lift my hand to my mouth. That scoundrel got into my head. "I don't know what that means, Signor Angeli. I live in New York, too. That suits me fine."

I gaze at the floor and take a cautious step forward. We're minutes from marrying. A wife needs to set rules and boundaries. Just because he's powerful doesn't mean I want to be governed. And my mind certainly isn't open for constant inspection.

"Listen...I think we..." My words trail off when he wraps a mighty arm around my waist and slams me into his chest. I gasp in surprise and crick my neck to gaze into his fiery steel eyes.

"We have no secrets, Livia. Don't close your mind to me and I won't close mine to you." He presses his plump lips to mine and takes my labored breath away. My knees weaken and I dig my hands into his hard pecs, gifting my fingertips with the delectable sensation.

He pulls away. "And this nun act ends today. You don't fool me, little girl. You rode Lucifer's cock mid air last night. If there was a hell, you would have earned your place."

I gasp and jump backward, clutching my mother's crucifix. "Luca! You know you had me under one of your spells." I turn away and fold my arms over my chest.

How dare he throw that it my face! I was lost in the heat of passion. Besides, we were already engaged.

His brow creases. He knows I'm lying. "You don't want to know the things I'll make you do under one of my spells, Livia. Lie again and find out."

A door swings open and Father O'Brien steps out. "Miss De Lucio? Mr. Angeli? Are you ready?"

Lucifer quirks his head and smiles. "Are you ready?"

I straighten my shoulders and walk ahead. "You don't scare me, mister. I've seen you cry."

22
LUCIFER

I LOOK OVER MY SHOULDER AND GLANCE AT THE STEEPLE. YOU CAN'T be too careful when it comes to archangels. They can't be trusted. Everyone thinks of childish cherubs playing lutes and guardian angels singing colicky babies to sleep. Those are not archangels. Those are new angels.

New angels are unblemished souls with innocent hearts like Livia. They cherish their work. They grow attached and weep for the loss of each one of their charges. Like Samael's little friend, Calla.

Two weeks ago, they tasked Samael with delivering a nine-year-old girl to heaven. Her body was weak. She'd lived a short miserable existence full of sickness and pain, but through it all, Calla held vigil. From the moment her little girl took her first breath to the moment she breathed her last, Calla stood by her side and prayed that someone would find a cure. But that cure never came.

Samael came.

When he arrived, Calla pleaded for more time. She knew the rules. She knew the decision wasn't his. He's a messenger—a courier of souls. But he broke the rules and gave Calla an extra hour with her girl. In that hour, they fell in love. She hasn't forgiven him for doing his job, but he swears they're in love.

Who knows? Maybe they are.

When you live in darkness, it's easy to appreciate the light. To Samael, Calla's light shone as bright as heaven. I know how that feels. Livia could light up the sky.

Archangels are different. They're Sephardim. The most powerful angels God created, and all power corrupts.

Look at what happened to me? They created me to believe I was the most beautiful, brightest and most loved of all the archangels. It was drilled into me for thousands of years. There was little surprise when it went to my head.

My brothers have spent their entire lives in the brightest halls of heaven. For them, there are no nuances. They don't question commands. They've killed innocent first-born sons. Delivered the wrath of God through plagues and destroyed cities.

If they believe Livia needs to die, they'll stop at nothing to make it happen. If they can destroy me, then they'll happily kill two birds with one stone.

"This feels dangerous, Livia. We can give this a few more days. I've sent Samael for more information." I squeeze her hand as we walk through the convent. She can't disguise her impatience with me. As she turns her head, I catch an obvious eye roll.

I've got it coming. I refused to let her fly. We showered together. When she insisted on having lunch in Paris before our drive to Saint Denis, I demanded she let me sample her food first. I'll surely drive her crazy before the end of the day.

"We've been married eight hours. I can still annul you." She marches ahead and hands our credentials to the Abbess. "Mother, my name is Madame Livia De Lucio. This is Monsieur Luca Angeli. We're here on behalf of Cardinal Bertolucci. Are the sisters ready for us?"

She looks us up and down and then politely nods, ushering us into a room where six nervous-looking nuns sit side by side behind a long wooden table. Behind them, with his hands on his hips and his wings unfurled, stands the Archangel Michael.

Livia freezes, then steps into my chest. "Who is that? He's huge." She squeaks like a kitten.

"Michael." I hold her in place and stare him down. "He wants to talk to me. He promises you'll be safe with the nuns while we speak."

She trembles in my arms and turns to face me. "How do you know he's not lying? What if I have a stroke?" She kisses my chin discreetly and wipes a tear from the corner of her eye. "I love you, Lucifer. If it's my time, it's my time. I'll try to be brave."

"Shut your mouth, Livia. Don't you dare leave with anyone. Don't you dare leave me in this fucked up world alone." I kiss her forehead and leave her to the nuns.

23
LIVIA

"What are you looking at?" I smile wide and tug the sheet to my chest. The sticky afterglow of sex still clings to my skin.

"I'm looking at my wife. The most beautiful woman in the room." Lucifer's eyes sparkle with love as he pulls me into his embrace and wraps his arms tightly around my back. With my face in his chest, I breathe in his scent, a combination of musk, embers and sage. It thrills me with the thought of every memory we've made together. He's sublime.

"I'm the only woman in the room, unless you see someone I don't. And if you see someone watching us make love, I hope you send them packing." I fake a pout and run a finger down his sculpted abdomen, following each line like a maze. His full lips creep into a wicked smile that tempts my fluttering heart.

One week of wedded bliss and I can't get enough of this beautiful man. I know what he is. It's hard to accept but I don't see evil. I don't see impenetrable darkness. I see more light shining through his spirit every day. Since our wedding, his wings have lightened and now look as gray as his heartbreakingly beautiful eyes.

I know there's good in him. I know he's not beyond redemption. Maybe he found me for a reason. If my love heals his pain, then the world might heal too. Without Lucifer's wrath, perhaps things will get better.

Know what I mean? It's possible.

Oh Lord, am I delusional? Please don't let me be like those women who write love letters to serial killers in prison!

"Hey! Where did you go?" He lifts my chin and kisses the top of my head.

I blink out of my daze and reach for the first thing in my grasp. "I was wondering how you get so hard so fast. We just made love." I smooth my palm along his stiff erection and buy myself some time. He knows I'm stalling. He's always hard. This is a nonsense question.

"Who are you? What did you do with my wife?" He chuckles, grips my shoulders and drags me up. "You're sweaty, naked and reek of sex, of course I'm fucking hard."

Before I can speak, he brings his lips to mine and I quickly lose myself in his kiss. Our hearts beat as one. His eager mouth demands my surrender and I'm helpless to do anything but submit. My fierce love makes me weak. My lust turns me wild.

When his mouth finds my tight nipples, I gasp and urge him on, arching my back against the mattress and smashing his face against the supple flesh of my breasts.

His hot breath makes me whimper. His teeth make me scream. Pain mixes deliciously with pleasure, just as love mixes with lust. With a hard thrust, he claims my tight pussy, slamming into me with the tenderness of a mating bull.

I lift my hips to meet his, thrashing with glee, and loving his brutal love as much as I enjoyed his gentler side an hour ago. He is an angel of many talents.

"I love you, Livia." He groans and seals his body to mine, radiating a fiery blue flame into my soul that flickers and spreads to every part of my being. With every thrust, his divine friction makes me wetter, as my body aches for more. My breath catches with every plunge. My heart thunders as the tension between us builds to greater heights. I can't get enough. I'll never get enough. Our savage lust knows no bounds.

"Lucifer! Please!" I don't know what I'm pleading for. I want more. I want to come. I want a baby. I want him to make the ache go away. Wailing without restraint or care, I arch my back and meet each plunge, whimpering with joy as this beautiful man breaks me in two.

When I near the edge of collapse or eternal ruin, his lips seize mine and his hands mercilessly knead the sensitive flesh of my breasts. He plunges harder, deeper, and yet my body wants so much more.

"I'll always be with you, Livia. I promise, my love. I'll love you until the end of time." He clasps my hands and pulls them over our heads. With slow, deep thrusts, his eyes lock on mine and a part of his spirit vibrates into my bones. My body shivers and my eyes fly open before a rush of unspeakable peace flows through me.

Without a word, the world goes black.

24

LUCIFER

I take a long look at Livia lying in bed and try to memorize every angle of her exquisite face. I love the tiny auburn freckles that line the bridge of her nose. Her long dark lashes always made her soft blue eyes appear brighter in contrast. I wish I could gaze into them one more time.

I take a deep breath and feel my heart slow to an imperceivable thump. If only I could make it stop beating. If I die, this could all end now.

With Michael standing nearby, I brush my mouth on her plump pink lips then gently kiss her forehead. While I linger, I inhale the scent of her skin and soak her cheeks with tears I can't restrain. I don't know how to walk away. All I want to do is crawl into her skin and stay with her forever. But I can't.

They gave me one week.

One week to be her husband. One week to live a life of unmitigated joy with the only woman I've ever loved.

But that's all they gave me. Not one day more.

If I walk away from Livia, she gets to live a full life. She gets to grow old. She wants a family. She wants a home and children. I hate this world. But through her eyes, I saw its possibilities. And I want her to live the life she wants.

Even if it's not with me.

In exchange, I surrender all hope of redemption. I passed on whatever light still lived in me to keep her safe. She's my wife. It's my responsibility to keep her from harm.

This was the only choice. If we stay together, she continues to live on borrowed time. At any moment, they can steal her away. But every day she evades her fate, she compromises her future.

She's guaranteed paradise now. The longer she stays with me, the more she jeopardizes her soul. I don't want her to return to a life of struggle and pain.

I'll bear my grief. For Livia, I'll bear anything.

Michael interrupts my thoughts. "I'm shocked you chose this path."

"Not another word or I'll strangle you." I choke on my tears, too devastated to care who sees me cry.

Pushing him away, I crawl onto the bed once more and curl her into my arms. While I weep openly, I explain my departure and beg her forgiveness. She won't remember me right away. I'll return in waves like bits and pieces of an insignificant event.

I don't want to be forgotten. But I want her to make new memories with the rat bastard who's lucky enough to win her heart.

And one day, many years from now, she'll remember Lucifer loved her.

"Let's go." I wipe my tears, kick Michael in the back and fly off the ledge.

25

EPILOGUE- THREE WEEKS LATER
LUCIFER

"You look like hell." Michael stands behind me, perched on a stone lion as I watch Livia scurry up the steps into the New York Public Library. She once told me this was her happy place. Every night she looks for books and finds a comfortable chair to read for a few hours. Today marks three weeks. Three weeks since I've held her in my arms. And three days since she returned to New York.

When she came home, I came home. I can't leave her side. I tried and could only bear it for minutes. It hurts too much to be apart from her.

"Why wouldn't I look like hell? Come, tear out my heart. If you kill me, you'll put me out of my misery. If I survive, at least I won't have to feel this torture every day until the end of time." I reach up and knock him down.

"You don't really love with your heart. You love with your brain. And with your soul. It just feels like your heart." He corrects me.

I bang my head into the sculpture. "Why are you here? There are no rules against me watching her from a distance. I haven't approached her. I'm not meddling in her life. And save your lectures about my unhealthy attachment. I told you I was in love with her. I gave up the one thing I wanted. No, the one thing I thought I wanted."

I grab the front of his robes and shake him.

"I wanted Livia more than redemption. More than anything. Please, kill me, Michael. Do your brother a favor and kill me. Put me out of my misery. Don't bring me back. Snuff my life out and let the ashes burn out forever." Clutching my broken heart, I fall to my knees, cling to the lion's feet and sob like the broken fool that I've become.

"For God's sake, Lucifer. You're making a scene." Michael tries to lift me.

I shake my head and bear down. "Stop acting like people can see me."

"I can see you and you're making me uncomfortable. Besides, you'll want to know why I've come." He taps my shoulder in a hollow gesture of sympathy.

I peek through my hands. "What? Why have you come? Why are you here?"

"When you asked for redemption, I said you didn't deserve it. In seven thousand years you'd never performed one selfless act." He smirks and stuff his hands in his pockets. I never realized those robes had pockets.

"And?" I don't get where he's going, but this build up is infuriating.

His brow creases. "Livia was a test. Livia was always meant to be a test. Father's planned this for ages. You were always meant to find her."

"Excuse me?" My mouth hits the pavement.

My Livia was a test?

They tested me?

I'm not sure how I feel about this.

"Personally, I never believed you'd fall in love. You're way too in love with yourself. Raphael was certain you wouldn't save her.

He said you'd let Lionel kill her. Gabriel swore you'd save yourself when things became complicated. None of us thought you'd sacrifice your own redemption for her. That blew our minds! But do you know who believed in you?" He pauses and waits for me to answer.

"Who?" I'm genuinely curious.

"Father did. He said you'd do all of it for her. He said love and only love would redeem you. And he was right. So now you get both." He offers me his hand.

"What? What does that mean? I get Livia? I can marry Livia? Are you pulling my leg?" I mumble in a state of confusion.

"You get both, Lucifer. Live a good mortal life with Livia. Grow old, raise your family and earn your redemption together. Good luck, brother." He pats my back and turns to leave.

"Wait, a minute! Who the hell am I? Where do I live? I don't have a job or identification." I panic. I don't have a cent to my name. I need to take care of Livia.

He chuckles. "Luca Angeli sounds right. You've got three days before you lose your wings. Make all the preparations you need. After that, we'll see you in seventy years."

"Seventy?!" I snap. After seven thousand years, seventy feels like a drop in the hat.

"Don't press your luck, Lucifer. Have a nice life, brother." He winks and fades away.

* * *

LIVIA

Winter came early and I fear I'm not prepared. Cold doesn't suit me. It's my fault. I doubted the forecasts. It seemed implausible. Two days ago, Central Park was bursting with fall splendor and the crisp November breeze I look forward to all year. Sleet feels shocking.

This is depressing, but I won't let it get me down.

Buzzing through the crowded sidewalk, I duck my head, pull my hat over my ears and follow a horde of afternoon commuters into the subway station. It's a short but welcomed reprieve from the frigid air. Soon I'll be home for two entire days of nothing.

And if I play my cards right, I won't need to emerge from hibernation until Monday.

It's been a bear of a week, but thanks to Cardinal Bertolucci's connections, I won't need to return to Rome until after the new year. He's made it possible for me to work out of the Diocese in New York through December. I told him it wasn't necessary, but he's a kind man and he's concerned for my health.

The good thing is Bishop Moore's candidacy is thoroughly quashed. The last three weeks were hell, but we worked overtime to bring his horrible actions to light. If they could have posthumously excommunicated him, they would have. Good riddance.

I admit my memory lapses had become embarrassing. First, I couldn't remember a man I met on a plane who ended up being murdered, and then I vaguely remembered the investigator who worked with me in Ireland. Some Luke character, I guess. Anyway, it's not important. I've got a great memory for things that matter. Sister Odette worries too much.

When physicians couldn't find anything wrong, they concluded it must be stress due to overwork. I think they're overreacting, but if it keeps me in New York through the holidays, I'll go along with the doctor's orders.

Lately, Rome's lost its sparkle. It used to be such a happy place. I could walk the streets, while I people-watched and window-shopped for hours. Not anymore. Everywhere I went felt like something or someone was missing. It was the oddest thing. I never fell in love, but somehow, I felt heartbroken.

Maybe the negativity from this last case seeped into my psyche. Depression runs in my family. I take a deep breath and try to stay positive.

Shake it off, Livia.

As I descend into the lower level, grumbles greet me on the platform. The anger is palpable. It's Friday afternoon. Almost everyone present is on their way home. There's no need to spiral into rage. The drop in temperature might be premature, but we're two weeks away from Thanksgiving and the official start of the holiday season.

I keep my optimism in check. No one's in the mood for it.

Clutching my bags against my body for warmth, I watch the incoming train skid to a noisy stop. It's packed and no one wants to make room for the rest of us. This always gets ugly.

As soon as the doors slide open, I charge into the crowded car and worm my way towards a rail. I just need something to hold. I'm not looking to sit down. Two stops and I can bust free from this can of sardines.

When the train whizzes out of the station, I slink into my small space and try to appear inconspicuous.

"Livia." A familiar whisper startles me. The chilly car grows warm and panic floods as his voice floats through the air and charges it with a quiet electricity. I turn my back and pretend I hear nothing.

Who is that? I know that voice. I know, I know it. I know I've heard it before. A faint glow of light rains comfort and my fear subsides.

Minutes later, I hear the sound of fluttering wings and my heart crashes into my sternum. Sweating profusely, I tear off my hat and scoot towards the end of the car.

I am going crazy. This happened to my father. I always thought I could beat, but maybe not.

Just in the nick of time, the train jolts to a stop and the doors slide open. I jump out a station early, fly through the crowd and crash straight into the chest of a gorgeous dark-haired man.

"Oh my goodness! Excuse me." I slink down, embarrassed by my clumsiness, and dash away. "Miss!" He calls out. Something in his voice startles me, but I keep running, scared out of my wits and desperate to get home.

* * *

It's too cold to head to the library. Fortunately for me, I've stocked up on books and groceries. I lick my finger and hold it in air. This feels like an exciting evening at home. Much like all my other exciting evenings at home.

I laugh to myself.

Fresh out of a hot bath, I pin my hair high and throw another log on the fire. The sight of the flames triggers a faint memory. It feels unreal. Gratuitous. No, *nasty*. But I've never had sex.

Have I? No, I'd know, for crying out loud. Maybe, I read about this in a book.

Wait a minute. My period's late. Why am I late? I'm never late. I'm two weeks late. It doesn't make any sense.

I rub my forehead, march into my bedroom and grab my work bag. There's no need to check my calendar. This is not something that needs double verification. I know my body.

I flip through reports and stacks of scattered notes, pull out my tablet, switch it on then tap open my calendar app. Yep, two weeks late. There was no need for verification.

This must be a fluke. *Oh Jesus, Cancer?*

No, I'm sure it's a fluke. I'll make an appointment on Monday. It can't be cancer. Why does my mind always jump to the worst possible scenario?

Now that I've effectively gone from zero to one hundred on the anxiety spectrum, I drag my feet back into the kitchen and turn on the stove. I'm starving. I've been hungry all day. Yesterday too. A sudden case of early menopause? Toilet seat pregnancy? Did I read that somewhere?

I slap my face. *Snap out of it, psycho.* You're just late!

My breath calms. Women are late all the time. It's no big deal.

LUCIFER

I'm almost back from the ledge when a sudden pound at the door sends me clear out of my skin.

Oh, my goodness. Who on earth is visiting me at 8:00pm on a Friday night?

I check my jammies in the mirror. They're decent for pajamas. *Nothing revealing.* But just to be safe, I grab my robe.

"Who is it?" I call out before I get close.

"Livia. It's me." The deep voice on the other side of the door winds its way into my heart and instantly untangles my brain.

For five seconds, the world stops. Luca.

I married a man named Luca. Luca Angeli.

But he's not Luca. He's Lucifer. Oh no, he's Lucifer.

Lucifer...LUCIFER. Dear Lord, I married Satan.

Wait, wait. He saved me. He saved me twice.

I touch my lips and remember the sweet taste of his kiss.

Lucifer loves me.

And I love him.

Memories rush back. Tears flood. Trembling with happiness, I swing open the door and jump into his arms.

"Livia!" Our eyes meet. Our lonely lips crash.

We'll never be apart again.

OH MY GOD, I'm pregnant.

26
EPILOGUE - 5 YEARS LATER
LUCIFER

"Cute dog." Asmodeus laughs while he watches me walk Frank Sinatra, Livia's blue-eyed Chihuahua.

I raise an eyebrow. "Don't annoy me. I'm walking my wife's dog. I love her and she loves him. End of fucking story. Why are you here?"

"We're family now. Livia's like my great great great great something or other. I don't know. Maybe your kids look like me." His voices carries a hint of sincerity but only a hint.

"I have incredibly attractive children. They look nothing like you." I lift Frankie off the ground and walk the tree-lined pathway overlooking Rome. "Why are you really here?"

"When you left Samael in charge I became his second. Now he wants to leave. Lucifer, I don't want to be in charge. What the shit am I going to do? Now Azazel is thinking of bailing." He wrings his hands and scowls.

"Why is this my problem? I'm not an angel anymore. My only power is sight." I look over my shoulder and see Livia headed our way. I know she can see him, but I'm not entirely sure if our oldest daughter can. We're still trying to figure it out. He's not the kind of angel I want her around. Even if he is a relative.

"You started this. You fell in love. Then Samael fell in love. Everyone saw you happy with a wife and kids and now Samael thinks he wants a slice of that pie. But I'd like to get in on that action, too! I'm not going to be left out in the cold." He huffs and folds his arms on his chest.

"You? You screw anything that moves. Who are you settling down with?" I keep my eye on Livia and gesture for him to hurry. I don't want the girls to hear all about Asmo's seedy exploits.

"I've got prospects." He shrugs and bristles with anger.

"Not the student teacher? The asthmatic? Glasses? You nearly killed her. Besides, that was years ago." I shoo him away as Livia approaches with our daughters.

He shakes his feathers. "She's a real teacher now. And I like the glasses. You're not the only one who likes substance, Lucifer." He gives me a dumb salute and flies away.

"What did he want?" Livia greets me with a kiss and hands me one of our daughters. Two-year-old Lucia looks just like her daddy. Gray eyes, black hair and a wicked disposition. Fortunately for us, she's inherited no abilities or she'd be a holy terror. Four-year-old Leah, is the spitting image of her mother and the perfect angel. We're divinely blessed. Even Frank Sinatra is a perfect gentleman and the apple of Livia's eye.

"Asmo doesn't want to take over. No one does. I've left a giant void." I take her hand and walk her to the ledge overlooking the city. We come to the Orange Garden every other weekend when the weather permits. This was Livia's fondest dream and it's my duty to make them all come true.

"Do you ever miss it?" She leans into my chest and gazes up with the pale blue eyes that first stole my heart.

"Not one second." I kiss her forehead.

"All my life I was afraid of the darkness and yet, that's where I found you. You saved me." Her misty eyes twinkle in the setting sun.

I shake my head and pull her closer. "I was saved the moment I fell in love with you."

THANKS FOR READING!

FOLLOW ME

Matilda loves many things---her husband, dachshunds, cats, the two terrible Chihuahuas who live with her, Paris, New York, a few select friends and family, Nutella, books, lots and lots of books, and writing sweet, steamy romance for nerdy girls-- because that's who I am.

If you like your romances steamy but sweet. Sexy, but on the shorter side. With smart and sassy heroines who fall for soulful Alphas- then you might like my books.

I write A LOT of OMYW, cause that's just my bag. But no matter what kind of story it is, my ladies are always adored and my endings are always HEA.

Please head to my blog to learn what's in the final stages and will be coming out soon!

ALSO BY MATILDA MARTEL

Love Unleashed

Leo Moretti always gets whatever he wants. No questions. He's his father's son and the blood in his veins is enough to make people fear the consequences of disappointing him.

Except Alia de Alba.

Alia's bold, beautiful and audacious. Her refusal has him on edge. When she turns down his marriage proposal, he incurs her wrath by playing the hero and manipulating her into marriage.

She wants to make him pay, but his hotness makes it hard. He swears they're soul mates but fears she loves someone else.

Can Leo win her heart?

Of course, he can. Leo Moretti always gets whatever he wants

This slow burn turned torrid affair includes one Sassy Latina, one hot Sicilan mafioso, love, lust, sexy times, various Pavarotti references, kidnappings, mobsters, two people who fall madly in love and a guaranteed happily ever after.

Love Interrupted

Igor Ivanov is a mob lawyer who's fallen head over heels in love with a senator's daughter.

Charlotte Wentworth is a Park Avenue princess who's in way over her head.

Madly in love, they defy their families and elope.

But after three blissful days, everything implodes, favors are called in and the two desperate lovers are torn apart.

Powerless and clueless, they part ways and spend four miserable years apart.

When a heartbroken Charlotte is finally allowed to come home, she wants answers. When Igor learns the truth, he wants things made right and more than anything he wants his Charlotte back.

He let her go once, he won't make that mistake again.

Can he convince Charlotte he's the same man she fell in love with? Or will four year of secrets, lies and threats tear them apart again?

This is a steamy second chance romance with two soul mates who fight the odds and crawl their way back home. Grab a cookie, sit into your favorite chair and meet Charlotte and Igor. As always, no cheating and a guaranteed happily ever after!

Filthy Love

Bella Hamilton is on a mission. Her best friend, Ava, is about to marry, and her surprise nuptials have thrown Bella's long-scheduled BFF plans for marriage and babies out of whack.

Never fear, Bella has a plan. She always has a plan. An interview with a young, hot billionaire is the golden opportunity she needs. And since she has no experience with men, she plans to use everything she's learned from years of reading romance novels to lure him into her web.

What on earth could go wrong?

Jude McCormick is nothing like his older brother. He doesn't believe in marriage. He doesn't yearn for a family. He goes from woman to woman and the only thing he longs for is escaping the yoke of his family's legacy.

But then he meets Bella. He's instantly attracted, but she dismisses him. He tries to flirt, but she reacts with disgust. She drives him crazy with lust, but she won't give him the time of day.

At the end of his rope, he's forced to take a harder look and the more he learns about this strange girl, the faster he falls in love.

Dirty, filthy love.

If you've ever wondered what it might be like if your significant other took cues from your favorite book boyfriends—you might like this novella!

Filthy Love is book two of a standalone series. This is an insta-love steamy romantic comedy and as always, this book contains sexy times, a happily ever after and no cheating!

Filthy Rich

Declan McCormick is filthy rich. He's gotten everything he ever wanted, but always wanted the wrong things. At thirty-eight, he's single, works seventy hours a week and comes home to an empty house every night.

Something needs to change.

Ava Jameson has come to New York to finish school. With rich parents, she's gotten everything she ever wanted, except their time. But she swears to do things differently. She has big dreams and one of those dreams is building a better family than her own.

When their paths cross, sparks fly. Declan charges full speed ahead but soon discovers the love of his life isn't so easily impressed and isn't interested in being the heroine of her own billionaire romance.

This is a short, sweet and steamy, insta-love contemporary, older man younger woman, billionaire romance novella with two people who quickly learn the best things in life never have a price tag. Enjoy!

Play Right

Shut Up & Kiss Me

Maestro

Lucky Man

Clever Girl

Magic Man

Agreeably Arranged

There She Goes

The Perfect Nanny

A Hostile Takeover

The Good Girl

The Pastor

The Trophy Wife

My Dad's Best Friend

My Fake Husband

Queen of Two Hearts

Closing Daddy's Deal

The Girl Next Door

And many more!

For updates on new releases click here and a free ebook, click here: www.matildamartel.com

Printed in the USA
CPSIA information can be obtained
at www.ICGtesting.com
LVHW042143151024
793932LV00028B/275

9 798201 870676